Research Skills

Three

James McCafferty

Deputy Headteacher of Holne Chase Combined School, Milton Keynes

Illustrated by Gillian Martin

Edward Arnold

© James McCafferty 1986

First published in Great Britain 1986 by
Edward Arnold (Publishers) Ltd
41 Bedford Square, London WC1B 3DQ

Edward Arnold (Australia) Pty Ltd
80 Waverley Road, Caulfield East
Victoria 3145, Australia

Reprinted 1986

British Cataloguing in Publication Data

McCafferty, James
    Research skills
    3
    1. Research — Methodology
    I. Title
    001.4'2   Q180.55.M4

    ISBN 0-7131-7379-3

Acknowledgements

I should like to thank the staff and children
of Stoke Park Junior School, Bishopstoke,
Hampshire, for trying out the rough draft of
this book in their own classes — my special
thanks to Ann Woodruff who spent so many
hours typing the draft.

J. McCafferty

The Publishers would like to thank the
following for permission to include copyright
material:

Macdonald Educational for material from
Patrick Rooke: *Peoples of the Past Series:
The Normans*, R J Unstead: *Invaded Island*,
Francis Coleman: *Great Britain*, Gavin Orton:
Scandinavia; Hamlyn Publishing for drawings
from Douglas Brown: *History Eye Witness
Series: Flyers*; Hampshire Bus Company
Limited for timetables; British Telecom for
material from Telephone Charges leaflet and
Code Book; British Rail and TrainLines of
Britain for timetables; Independent
Television Publications Ltd for a page from
the ITV and Channel Four programmes
listing; Radio Times for a page from their
programmes listing; The Automobile
Association and Ordnance Survey for
material from the 1980/81 AA Members'
Handbook and Ordnance Survey for a section
from Landranger Series Sheet 152.

Text Photoset in 12 point Univers by
Tek-Art, Croydon, Surrey
Printed and bound in Hong Kong by Wing King Tong Co Ltd

Contents

For Susi, Sara and Heidi

1 Information from pictures   2

A well-drawn picture can often save pages of explanation, because the reader can **see** the information that is being presented.

You can find a great deal of information about Norman knights and the warfare of that period in history by studying the picture on page 6.

Answer these questions:

1. What name is given to the knight's coat of mail?
2. What does the knight wear under his helmet?
3. What do the knight's feet rest in?
4. What protects the knight's face?
5. What shape is his shield?
6. What three weapons does he carry?
7. How is his helmet strengthened?
8. Why does the coat of mail have short sleeves?
9. Is his sword worn outside or inside the hauberk?
10. With which hand does the Norman control his horse?
11. What other control over his horse does he have?
12. How are his lower legs protected?
13. How is his shield attached to him?
14. Why is it such an unusual shape?
15. Is the Norman a cavalryman or an infantryman?

Study the picture of a Roman soldier on page 7, then answer the questions.

1. What is different about the labelling on this picture?
2. What is the Roman's helmet called?
3. Which two metals could it be made of?
4. What was the 'pilum' and how long was it?
5. What is the Roman's main armour made of?
6. Where is it hinged?
7. On which side does he wear his sword?
8. What other weapon does he wear?
9. Why does he wear a scarf?
10. What is his tunic made of?
11. What protection does he have for his face?
12. What made the Roman's leather sandals hard-wearing?
13. Why does he wear a wrist-guard on his left arm?
14. Why is his shield an unusual shape?
15. What material is it made of?

If you **compare** the picture of the Roman soldier with the picture of the Norman knight, you can begin to see some of the main differences in the way they fought. Look at **both** pictures and then answer these questions:

16. Which soldier wore most armour?
17. Why did the Roman not wear much armour below the waist?
18. Compare the use of the Norman lance and Roman pilum — were they designed to be used in the same way?
19. Why is the Norman's sword longer than the Roman's?

20. Which sword would be best as a stabbing weapon?
21. Which suit of armour was designed for use in hotter countries? How do you know?
22. Why would a hauberk not have been much help to a Roman soldier?
23. Why would a Roman shield not have been very useful to a Norman knight?
24. Which soldier would have had the most advantage in combat on foot? Why?
25. Why did the Romans not use a nasal on their troops' helmets?
26. Which soldier's weapons would have been used at a distance?
27. Which soldier's shield protected the largest part of his body?
28. Which 'last resort' weapon did each soldier use if his main weapons were broken?
29. Why would the Norman not have found the Roman's last resort weapon much use?

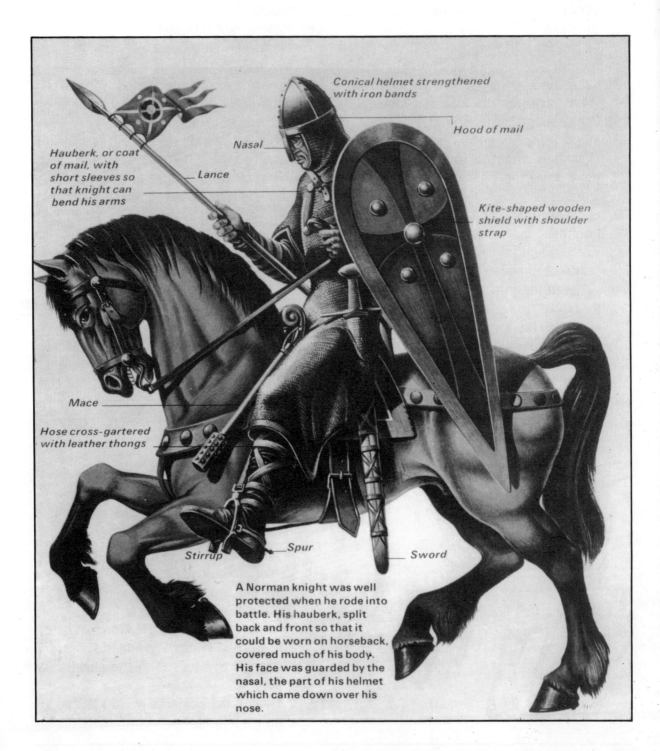

Conical helmet strengthened with iron bands

Hood of mail

Nasal

Hauberk, or coat of mail, with short sleeves so that knight can bend his arms

Lance

Kite-shaped wooden shield with shoulder strap

Mace

Hose cross-gartered with leather thongs

Stirrup

Spur

Sword

A Norman knight was well protected when he rode into battle. His hauberk, split back and front so that it could be worn on horseback, covered much of his body. His face was guarded by the nasal, the part of his helmet which came down over his nose.

30. Imagine a battle taking place between Norman knights and Roman infantry (it could never have happened really!) Write about the way in which their weapons would have been used against each other, and who you think might have won. Give your reasons.

The Roman Soldier

1 Helmet, made of either bronze or iron with leather cheek pieces. The Latin for helmet is *cassis*. A legionary would wear a badge on his *cassis* for ceremonial parades.

2 Armour, made of metal strips fastened together. The strips are curved around the shoulders and across the chest. They are laced in front and hinged at the back.

3 Tunic and scarf are worn to save skin from getting sore.

4 Heavy javelin, or *pilum*, 7 ft long, with pointed end to stick in ground. Each soldier carried two javelins.

5 Dagger, or *pugio*. This one measures from nine inches to ten inches.

6 Belts, tunics, boots, aprons and breeches are made of leather. Thongs of the apron have metal plates all the way down, and bronze weights on the end of each thong. Apron hangs from the belt.

7 Two-edged sword, or *gladius*: 2 ft long.

8 Shield made of sheets of wood with iron or bronze at the edges: held by a handgrip on the inside.

9 Boots, or heavy leather sandals, with metal studs on the soles.

3 Cutaway drawings

When you look at a picture of a machine, it may not be much help because the important details are often **inside**, where you can't see them. To help you understand how it works a **cutaway drawing** is used. This shows the outside of the object as if it were transparent – as if you could 'see inside it'. In this way, a cutaway drawing can save lots of writing. Look carefully at the cutaway drawings of two aircraft from World War Two.

Now answer these questions:

1. Which half of the Hurricane Mk I is drawn as if it were transparent?
2. Which wing of the Bf.109 E-3 is drawn as if it were transparent?
3. Use the information in the pictures to write TRUE or FALSE for each of these statements:
   a) Both aircraft are single-engined.
   b) Both aircraft have three landing wheels.
   c) Both aircraft are armed with machine guns.
   d) Ammunition is stored in the wings of both aircraft.
   e) The Bf.109 E-3 has a Rolls-Royce engine.
   f) Both aircraft are fitted with radios.
   g) Both aircraft are monoplanes.
   h) The Bf.109 E-3 has more guns than the Hurricane Mk I.

4. How many exhaust pipes are shown on each aircraft?
5. Do both aircraft's wheels retract in the same direction?
6. What does the Hurricane use to cool its engine?
7. What tells you that the Bf.109 could fly at a high altitude?
8. Which aircraft has the more powerful armament?
9. What safety feature is not shown in the Bf.109's cockpit?
10. What were both these aircraft designed as?

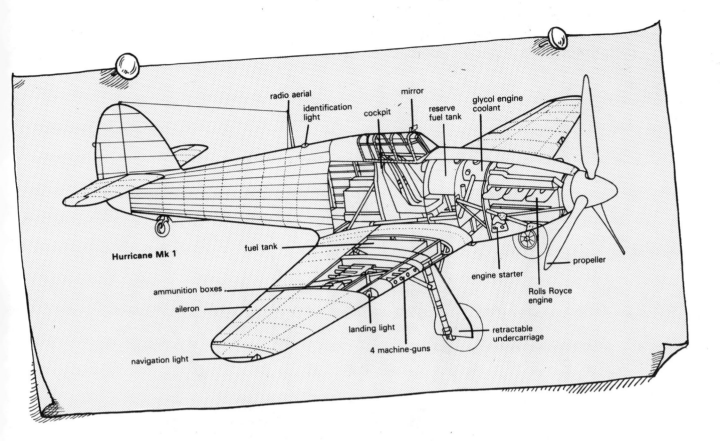

radio aerial

identification light

cockpit

mirror

reserve fuel tank

glycol engine coolant

Hurricane Mk 1

fuel tank

ammunition boxes

aileron

navigation light

landing light

4 machine-guns

engine starter

Rolls Royce engine

propeller

retractable undercarriage

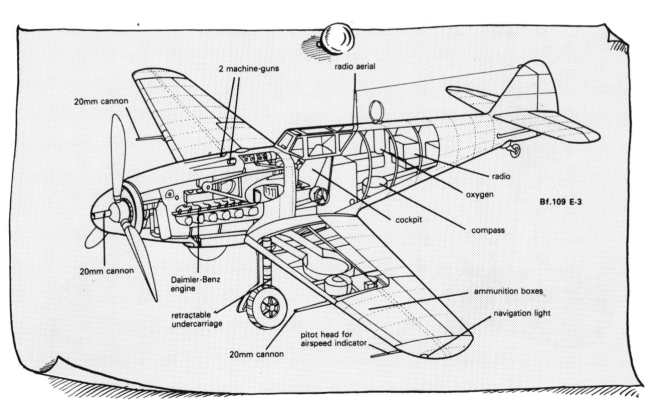

2 machine-guns

radio aerial

20mm cannon

radio

oxygen

Bf.109 E-3

cockpit

compass

20mm cannon

Daimler-Benz engine

retractable undercarriage

ammunition boxes

navigation light

pitot head for airspeed indicator

20mm cannon

4 Pictographs

A great deal of information can be shown in the form of a pictorial graph or **pictograph**. This is really a combination of a graph or pie chart and a set of pictures. Look at this pictograph showing how Britain compares with four other countries on ownership of cars, televisions and so on:

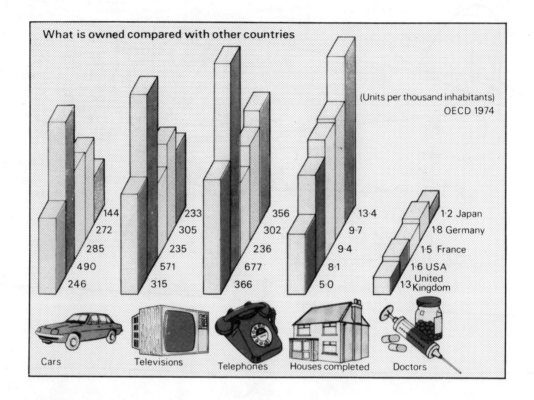

What is owned compared with other countries

(Units per thousand inhabitants)
OECD 1974

	Cars	Televisions	Telephones		
	144	233	356	13·4	1·2 Japan
	272	305	302	9·7	1·8 Germany
	285	235	236	9·4	1·5 France
	490	571	677	8·1	1·6 USA
	246	315	366	5·0	1·3 United Kingdom

Cars　Televisions　Telephones　Houses completed　Doctors

By a piece of clever drawing, the artist is showing you five separate bar graphs side by side, and the pictures underneath each graph show you what is being compared. The horizontal axis is actually on the right-hand side and gives the names of the five countries being compared.

Look at the information on the pictograph and answer these questions:

1. 'Units per thousand inhabitants' means the number of objects (cars, telephones, etc.) there are for every thousand people in each country. How many telephones are there for every thousand people in:
   a) Japan?
   b) Germany?
   c) France?
   d) USA?
   e) United Kingdom?

4. Look at the bar graph of doctors.
   a) Which country has most doctors per thousand people?
   b) Which country has fewest doctors per thousand people?
5. Which country owns more televisions than telephones?
6. Which country owns more cars than televisions?

2. Look at the bar graph of houses completed.
   a) Which country has the largest bar?
   b) Which country has the smallest bar?
   c) What does that tell you?
3. Which country has the largest bar in the:
   a) car graph?
   b) television graph?
   c) telephones graph?
   d) What does that information tell you?

7. In which two graphs is the UK near the top?
8. In which graph is the UK at the bottom?
9. a) Which country has the lowest ownership of cars and televisions?
   b) Why is that surprising?
10. a) Which country seems to have the most successful building industry?
    b) What is the evidence?

5

If a pictograph is about one particular country or group of countries, it can tell you a great deal, but you need to **interpret** the pictograph carefully.

Look at this pictograph about exports and imports in Scandinavia:

The Nordic countries: imports and exports, 1976 (includes Iceland)

EXPORTS:
- Food and live animals 4,400·8
- Meat and meat preparations 1,372·4
- Dairy products and birds eggs 691·6
- Fish and fish products 1,129·4
- Pulp and waste paper 1,893·2
- Mineral fuels, lubricants etc. 2,280·3
- Petroleum products 2,106·7
- Chemicals and related products 2,240·7
- Machinery and transport equipment 14,226·7
- Road vehicles 2,240·6
- Clothing 779·5

IMPORTS:
- Food and live animals 3,631·7
- Meat and meat preparations 176·8
- Dairy products and birds eggs 59·4
- Fish and fish products 350·3
- Pulp and waste paper 108·4
- Mineral fuels, lubricants etc. 8,301·6
- Petroleum products 7,467·3
- Chemicals and related products 3,888·8
- Machinery and transport equipment 16,607·3
- Road vehicles 3,541·1
- Clothing 1,587·9

Source: Yearbook of Nordic Statistics 1977

'Exports' means goods SOLD by a country. 'Imports' means goods that country has to BUY.

BRAIN BOX

Now answer these questions:

1. You are really looking at two bar graphs. What have they been made to look like?
2. Where has the information been gathered from?
3. How many different items are shown on each graph?
4. Why are the bars showing 'machinery and transport equipment' twice as wide as the others?
5. If a country exports (sells) more cars than it imports (buys) it has produced a TRADE SURPLUS. But if it imports more cars than it exports this is called a TRADE DEFICIT.

   Look carefully at the two pictographs and write **surplus** or **deficit** for each of these items:
   a) Clothing
   b) Pulp and waste paper
   c) Road vehicles
   d) Fish and fish products
   e) Food and live animals
   f) Petroleum products
   g) Meat and meat preparations
   h) Dairy products
6. Make a table like this one in your book:

7. In what **type** of goods do the Scandinavian countries have a trade deficit? Think of a general title for the **whole group** of items.
8. In what **type** of goods do the Scandinavian countries have a trade surplus?
9. Which item on the export graph is the largest?
10. What does this tell you about the kind of work that most people do in Scandinavia?

Scandinavian Exports and Imports

Trade surplus	Trade deficit

Write each of the 11 items shown in the pictograph in the correct column.

6 Comparing different graphs

Look at these two graphs of washing machine sales:

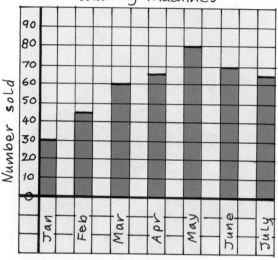

Graph A: Sales of automatic washing machines

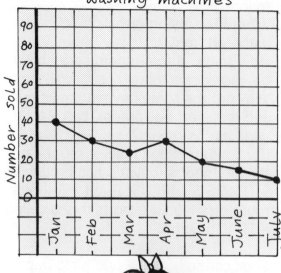

Graph B: Sales of twin-tub washing machines

1. Are the scales on the vertical axis of both graphs the same? (Sometimes people can fool you by using different scales to make one graph look bigger!)
2. What does 1 square on the vertical axis stand for?
3. Are sales in Graph A increasing?
4. Are sales in Graph B increasing?
5. In Graph A, how many automatic washing machines were sold in:
   a) January?
   b) February?
   c) March?
   d) April?
6. In Graph B, how many twin-tub machines were sold in the same months?
7. In Graph A, how many more automatics were sold in May than in January?
8. Why did automatic sales drop off in June and July?
9. In which month did twin-tub sales increase?
10. How many machines of **both** kinds were sold in February?
11. Which is easiest to read, the Bar Graph or the Line Graph?
12. Write one sentence to explain the **main idea** shown by the graphs.

7 Misleading graphs

Sometimes information is presented on a graph to make you believe someone's ideas.

Look at these two line graphs which show increases in prices and wages:

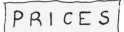

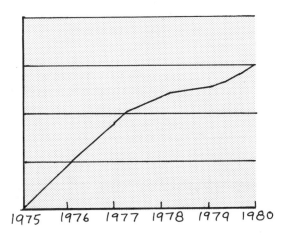

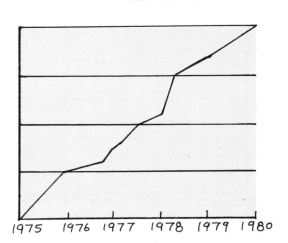

Now answer these questions:

1. Which have increased most, prices or wages?
2. In which of the two graphs does the sharpest increase occur?
3. Write TRUE or FALSE for each of these statements:
   a) After a sharp increase, prices are now levelling out.
   b) Wages increased a great deal between 1977 and 1978.
   c) In 1976 prices and wage increases were at about the same level.
   d) In 1980 wages were a long way ahead of prices.
   e) People are better off now than they were in 1976.
4. What is missing from both graphs?

5. Now look at both graphs again, with the missing information added:

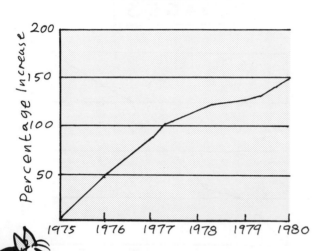

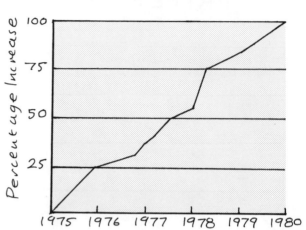

a) What do you notice about the vertical scales?
b) Draw both graphs on squared paper, using the same vertical scale of 1:25.

   What do you notice?

6. Was the information on the first two graphs false or true?

7. Look at your answers (a) to (e) in number 3, and then at the graphs you have drawn yourself.
   a) Write TRUE or FALSE for each statement again.
   b) Have your answers changed?

8 True and false graphs

British Nuclear Power Ltd want to build a nuclear power station near the village of Trevelyan in Cornwall. Some of the villagers object and say that most of the village is against it. British Nuclear Power Ltd carry out a survey (opinion poll) in the village and publish a statement in the local newspaper (shown on page 17).

**Look very carefully at each graph.
Read the four statements.**

1. Write **Statement A** in your book. Put TRUE or FALSE next to it, then explain why you think it is true or false.
   Now do the same for statements B, C and D.
2. a) Graph 1 makes the increase in jobs look very big. In which **two** ways does it do this?
   Draw Graph 1 again yourself, but use a new scale which begins at 0.
   b) What do you notice?

16

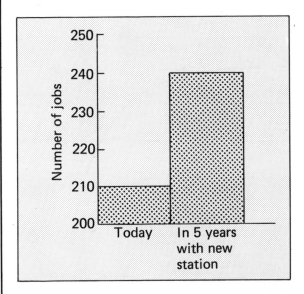

Graph 1: New jobs created by the Nuclear Station

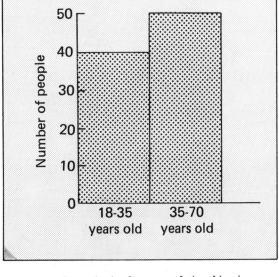

Graph 2: People in favour of the Nuclear Station

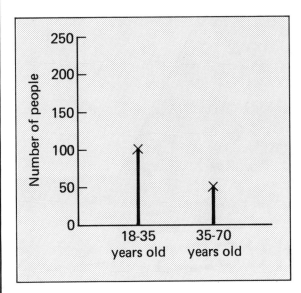

Graph 3: People against the new Nuclear Station

A. As you can see from Graph 1 above, our new power station will mean a large increase in the number of jobs for people in Trevelyan.

B. Graph 2 shows the large number of villagers who want us to build the new station, with rather more older people in favour.

C. Our third graph shows the number of those who are opposed to the station. It seems that more younger people are against the plan.

D. More older villagers are in favour of the new Nuclear Station.

Statement dated 4 March from British Nuclear Power Ltd.

3. Graphs 2 and 3 are correct, but they have been drawn in different ways to fool people. In which **two** important ways are they differently drawn?

4. a) How many young people are **for** the new station?

b) How many young people are **against** the new station?

c) Why doesn't this show up on the graphs?

d) What do you notice about the numbers of older people **for** and **against**?

5. If you only looked quickly at Graphs 2 and 3, what would you think the villagers felt about the Nuclear Station idea?

6. Which part of the graphs should you look at carefully **before** you make up your mind?

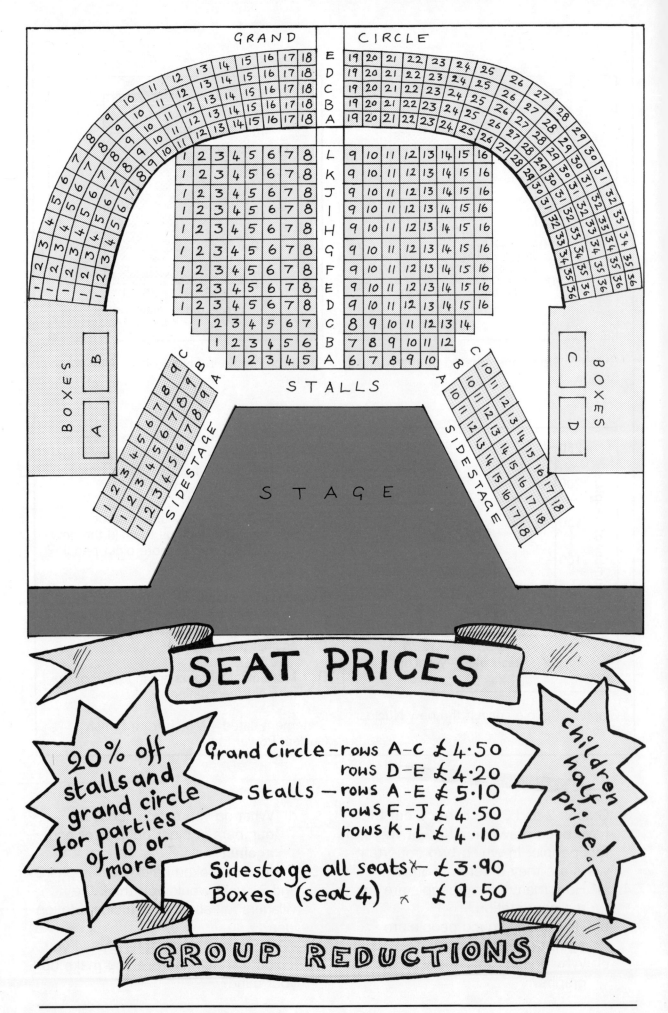

SEAT PRICES

20% off stalls and grand circle for parties of 10 or more

Grand Circle – rows A–C £4·50
rows D–E £4·20
Stalls – rows A–E £5·10
rows F–J £4·50
rows K–L £4·10

Sidestage all seats ✗ £3·90
Boxes (seat 4) ✗ £9·50

children half price!

GROUP REDUCTIONS

9 Reading a seating plan

A theatre seating plan is designed to help you choose the best seats for your money. Look at this theatre's plan and price list opposite.

Now answer these questions:

1. Why are the first three rows of the stalls the most expensive seats?
2. Which seats are the cheapest? Why?
3. How does it work out that the boxes are actually cheaper?
4. The seats are numbered with the row number, then the number of the seat (A1, A2 and so on).
   a) Which two seats in the stalls probably get the best view of all?
   b) Which two seats in the grand circle probably get the best view?
   c) Which two sidestage seats probably get the worst view?
   d) Which two boxes get the best view?
   e) Which two grand circle seats probably get the worst view?
5. How much would the following bookings cost?
   a) Two adults in box C.
   b) Three adults in stalls row G.
   c) Five adults in grand circle row D.
   d) Four adults in stalls seats E6, E7, F6, F7.
   e) Two adults in grand circle seats D25 and D26 and two children in the row in front.
   f) A party of twelve adults, half in stalls row K and half in sidestage row B. (Show your working-out.)
   g) Mr and Mrs Landon, with their three children in stalls row F.
6. Mike is sitting in grand circle A20 and drops his ice-cream over the balcony. Which seat does it land on?
7. Andrea and Claire are sitting in stalls J3 and J4 and notice two of their friends exactly five rows in front.
   a) What are their friends' seat numbers?
   b) How much more did their friends pay to get in?

8. Mum, Dad and their two children want to see the play on Saturday. Dad can only spare £12.50 for all their tickets. Unfortunately, the sidestage seats and boxes are booked. Which part of the theatre do they end up in?
9. A coach party of 35 adults and 10 children book the following seats:

   Adults: Stalls rows B and C (all seats)
             Sidestage row A (9 seats)
   Children: Stalls row A (all seats)

   Work out the total cost of their booking.
10. a) How many seats are there in the theatre? Don't count them all! Show your working-out.
    b) Saturday's play is a sell out. All the seats are sold to adults and there are no group reductions. Work out how much money the box-office took on Saturday. A calculator may save you some time!

10 Sketch plans

A diagram of how something looks **from above** is called a PLAN. Look at this plan of a classroom.

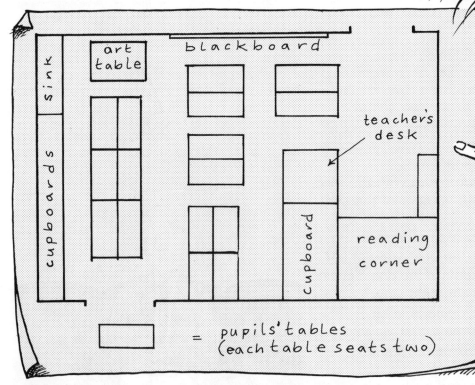

Now answer these questions in sentences:

1. If each table seats two children, how many children can sit down in class?
2. If there are 32 children in the class, how many spare places are there?
3. How many doors are there?
4. How many tables are in the biggest group?
5. What does the teacher sit next to?
6. Why do you think the art table is not in another corner?
7. The blackboard is between the _____ and the _____.
8. Where would you put bookshelves on this plan?
9. If each table is **1 metre** long, estimate in metres:
   a) the width of the doors
   b) the length of the blackboard
   c) the length of the cupboards near the sink
   d) the length of the whole room
10. What are most of the shapes in the plan called?

11

To make a sketch plan you don't need to measure anything. All you have to show is more or less where each thing is. On a sketch plan you **estimate** where things are and how big they are.

1. On scrap paper, make a sketch plan of your classroom.
2. Write **labels** to show what each thing is.
3. Show it to your teacher – you might have missed something!
4. Now make a neat copy of it in your book. Use a ruler for the straight lines.
5. What do you notice about most of the shapes on your plan?
6. Have you written a title at the top of your plan?

12 Scale

You have already used **scale** to draw the graphs you worked on earlier. Scale can also be used in plan-making.

Look at this plan of a school playground:

Scale: 1 cm : 5 m

The scale means that 1 centimetre on the plan stands for 5 metres on the real playground.

BRAIN BOX

1. How long is the **plan** of the playground? Use your ruler to check.
2. How long is the **real** playground?
3. How wide is the **plan** of the playground? Use your ruler to check.
4. How wide is the **real** playground?
5. a) What is the distance around the outside of the plan (its PERIMETER)? Use your ruler to check.
   b) What is the perimeter of the real playground?

13

Here is some practice in working out the
real lengths shown on a scale plan.
Measure these lines with your ruler and
write down the **real** lengths shown:

1. Scale 1 cm : 1 metre
   a) _____
   b) _____
   c) _____

2. Scale 1 cm : 10 metres
   a) _____
   b) _____
   c) _____

3. Scale 1 cm : 100 metres
   a) _____
   b) _____
   c) _____

4. Scale 1 cm : 10 kilometres
   a) _____
   b) _____
   c) _____

5. Scale 0   10   20   30   40   50   metres
   a) _____
   b) _____
   c) _____

6. Scale 0   20   40   60   80   100   kilometres
   a) _____
   b) _____
   c) _____

7. Scale 0   50   100   150   200   250   metres
   a) _____
   b) _____
   c) _____

8. Scale 0   200 400 600 800 1000   kilometres
   a) _____
   b) _____
   c) _____

*Centimetre
Snake !*

14 Scale plans

Look at this scale plan of Mrs Smith's

Scale plan of Mrs Smith's desk

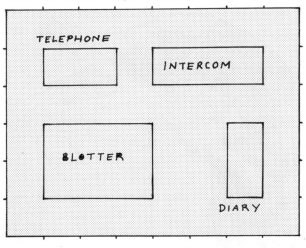

Scale : 1 cm : 10 cm

You can work out the **real size** of Mrs Smith's desk by using the scale.

1 centimetre on the plan stands for **10 centimetres** on the real desk.

Use the scale to work these out:

1. How long is the desk?
2. How wide is the desk?
3. How long is the telephone?
4. How long is the intercom?
5. What is the perimeter of the blotter?
6. How far away from the diary is the intercom?
7. What is the area of the blotter in square centimetres (cm^2)?
8. How far from the blotter is the diary?
9. What is the perimeter of the desk?
10. How big is the diary (length and width)?

15

Look at this scale plan of John's room:

Scale plan of John's room

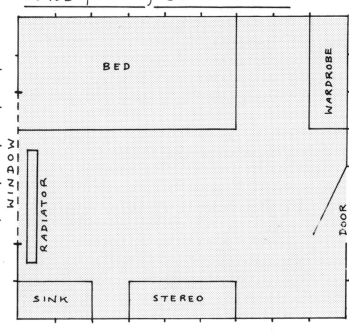

Scale : 1 cm : 40 cm

You can work out the **real sizes** and **distances** of things on this plan by using the scale.

The scale means that **1 centimetre** on the plan stands for **40 centimetres** in John's room.

Use the scale to work these out:

1. How long is John's room?
2. How wide is John's room?
3. How long is his bed?
4. How wide is his bed?
5. How much space is there between his bed and the wardrobe?
6. How long is the window?
7. How wide is the door?
8. Which way does the door open?
9. What size (length and width) is the sink?
10. How is the room heated?

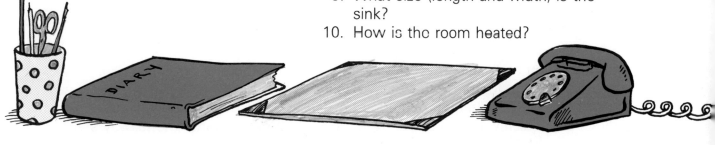

16

1. Make a **scale plan** of your desk or table on squared paper. Use a scale of **1 cm : 10 cm** (1 centimetre on the plan will stand for 10 centimetres on the real desk or table).
2. Show it to your teacher.
3. Practise making some other scale plans in different parts of your school.
4. Why couldn't you use the **same** scale for all your plans?

17 Finding your way round on a plan

A street plan is a set of information about a town. To find your way around you need to be able to 'imagine' your way into the plan.

Look at this plan of Sefton town centre:

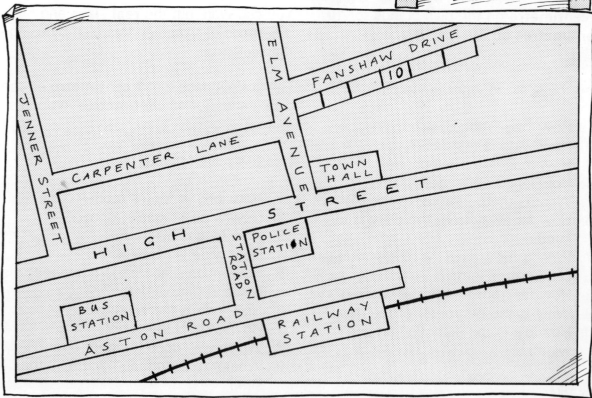

Suppose you have just arrived on the bus and want to get to 10 Fanshaw Drive. In your book write a clear, numbered set of directions which will take you there.

Here is the first one:

1. From bus station walk along Aston Road towards the railway station.

18

When you are writing a set of directions you have to be very clear about 'left' and 'right'. You can also use 'landmarks' like the Town Hall and Police Station in the town plan you have just been working on.

Write a clear, numbered set of directions to tell someone how to get from your classroom to the farthest classroom. Think carefully about the 'landmarks' you will include.

Discuss your directions with your teacher.

19 Street plans

For this exercise you will need a street plan showing the roads around your school and your home – or a very good memory!

1. Write a clear, numbered set of directions which tell someone how to get from your school to your house. Use the street names and include landmarks like shops, churches, telephone boxes and so on.
2. Draw a sketch plan of the area between your home and school. Mark the journey from school to your house in red.

See if your friend agrees with your directions – check for 'left' and 'right'!

20 Scale street plans

Look at this scale plan of a village:

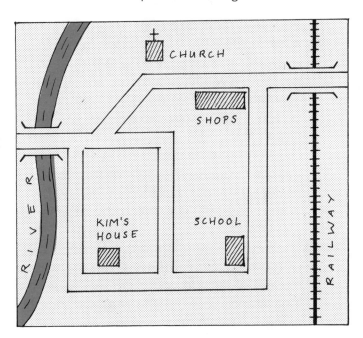

Scale : 1 cm : 100 metres

1. Draw the signs for:
   a) a bridge
   b) a railway line
   c) a church
2. To leave the village, Kim must cross over the _____ or the _____.
3. How far does Kim have to walk to school?
4. How far is it from the river bridge to the railway bridge?
5. What is the distance from the school to the church?
6. Kim wants to meet a friend at the railway bridge. Which way is quicker:
   a) the road past the church, or
   b) the road past the school?
7. How far is it in a straight line ('as the crow flies') from:
   a) the school to the church?
   b) the shops to Kim's house?
   c) the river bridge to the school?

21 Finding distances on a scale plan

Very few roads are really as straight and easy to measure as the ones in the last exercise. It is difficult to use a ruler to measure a winding road on a plan. It is more accurate if you use a piece of string or cotton. Here's how . . .

Hold one end of the string at the start of the road you are measuring, then carefully fit the string round all the curves and bends in the road until you reach the other end.

Then cut the string where it meets the end of the road. Straighten out the string and place it alongside your ruler. Measure its length and work out the **real** distance by using the scale on the plan.

Look at this scale map of part of the outskirts of Holmhurst:

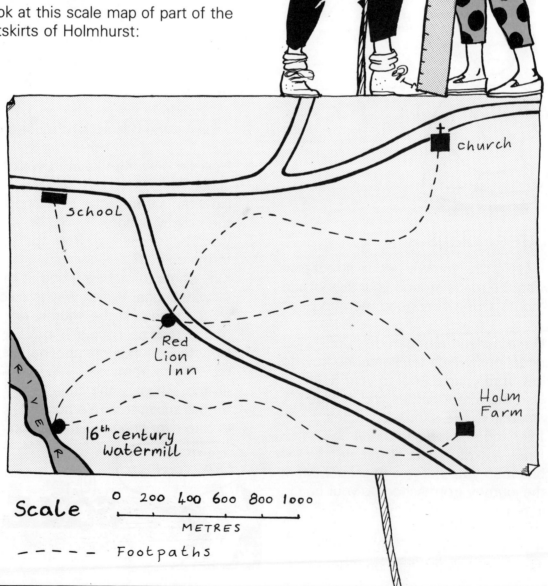

Scale

```
0   200  400  600  800  1000
|___|___|___|___|___|
        METRES
```

- - - - - Footpaths

1. Using cotton or string and the scale shown on the map, find the real distance you would walk if you used the footpaths to get from:
   a) the church to the 'Red Lion'
   b) Holm Farm to the watermill
   c) the school to Holm Farm

2. If an aircraft flew over the school and the church it would be travelling in a straight line. It would travel a shorter distance than a car, because a car would have to follow the bend in the road. This shorter distance, travelling directly in a straight line, is called **direct distance** or **'as the crow flies'**.

   Use your ruler to work out the direct distance between:
   a) the church and the watermill
   b) the school and Holm Farm

3. If an aircraft was flying at a speed of 40 m/sec (metres per second), work out:
   a) how long it would take to fly from Holm Farm to the school
   b) its speed in km/hr (kilometres per hour).
   Show your working-out.

22 Information from a timetable

Here are the different ways you can travel by air from Britain to the People's Republic of Polygonia:

Airline	Airport	Day	Flight No.	Stopover at
British Airways	Heathrow	M	BA 936	Munich
Air India	Heathrow		AI 740	—
Lufthansa	Gatwick		DL 613	Bahrain
KLM	Manchester	T	NK 824	Rome
Aeroflot	Heathrow		CC 142	Moscow
British Airways	Luton	W	BA 961	Frankfurt
Lufthansa	Gatwick		DL 745	Bahrain
KLM	Luton		NK 887	Zurich
Qantas	Heathrow	Th	QA 039	Bahrain
Air India	Heathrow		AI 788	—
British Caledonian	Gatwick		BC 106	Athens
British Airways	Heathrow	F	BA 979	Munich
Aeroflot	Gatwick		CC 202	Moscow
KLM	Manchester		NK 900	Rome

(All flight details fictionalised.)

Look at the information in the timetable, especially at the headings above each column, then answer these questions:

1. How many flights a week do these airlines make to Polygonia?
   a) KLM
   b) British Airways
   c) Aeroflot
2. On which days of the week do Lufthansa operate their service to Polygonia?
3. On which day are there fewest flights?
4. Which airports do these airlines use?
   a) KLM
   b) Air India
   c) Lufthansa
5. Which airlines use stopovers in these places?
   a) Frankfurt
   b) Rome
   c) Moscow

6. Which airline flies non-stop to Polygonia?
7. On which days do these flights operate?
   a) DL 745
   b) CC 202
   c) AI 740
8. From which airports do these flights operate?
   a) NK 900
   b) QA 039
   c) BC 106
9. Which airlines operate only one flight a week to Polygonia?
10. On which day of the week is there a service to Polygonia from three different airports?

23 Bus routes

Bus companies use maps to show the places they serve and the numbers of the buses which operate along the roads. The maps usually only show the roads served by the bus company. Buildings and other details are left off the service maps.

Look at the map on page 30 which shows bus routes in the Eastleigh area.

1. Write down the numbers of the buses which serve:
   a) Pitmore Road
   b) Brambridge Road
   c) Spring Lane
   d) Chestnut Avenue
   e) Sandy Lane
   f) Church Road
   g) Kingsway
   h) Leigh Road
2. In which street is the bus station?
3. The railway station is on the corner of two roads. Which ones?
4. Look at the direction taken by the railway lines. Which four towns are probably served by the railway?
5. Does the railway pass UNDER or OVER these roads?
   a) Twyford Road
   b) Brambridge Road
   c) Bournemouth Road
   d) Bishopstoke Road

As well as being shown on a route map, the Eastleigh area buses are also listed in an index in the bus timetable. Look at page 31.

6. Which buses serve:
   a) Whiteparish?
   b) Lower Upham?
   c) Crowd Hill?
   d) Stoke Common?
   e) Chilworth?
   f) Woolston?
   g) Moorgreen?
   h) Barton Stacey?

7. Which bus would you travel on if you were going from:
   a) Eastleigh to West End?
   b) Eastleigh to Romsey?
   c) Southampton to Otterbourne?
   d) Southampton to Hursley?
   e) North Baddesley to Eastleigh?
   f) Bishop's Waltham to Southampton?
   g) Hedge End to Eastleigh?
   h) Southampton to Farnham?
8. Look again at the bus route map and write TRUE or FALSE for each of these statements:
   a) The Stoke Common buses travel along Church Road.
   b) The bus to Allbrook travels along Brambridge Road.
   c) The bus from Bishopstoke to Pylehill goes via Alan Drayton Way.

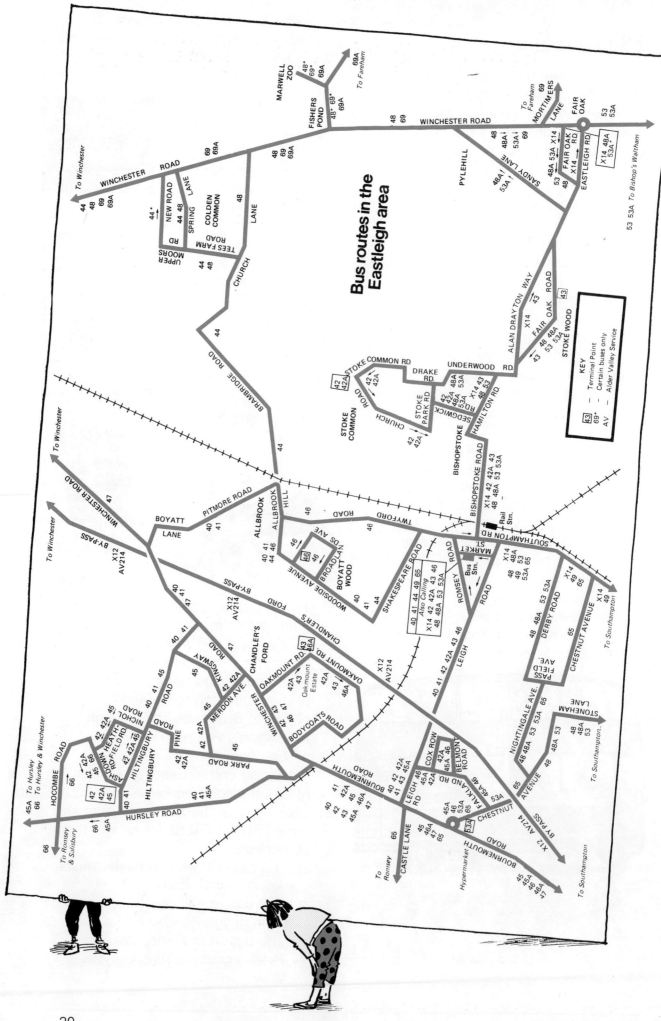

Bus routes in the Eastleigh area

KEY

43 — Terminal Point
69* — Certain buses only
AV — Alder Valley Service

30

WHICH BUS GOES WHERE?

CODE   ‡—Certain buses only.   *AV214*—Alder Valley Service.

Full details of services to certain places are shown in other timetable booklets:
- ●—See 'South Hants' (Bishop's Waltham) booklet.
- ♥—See 'South Hants' (Romsey) booklet.
- □—See 'Provincial' booklet.
- ■—See 'Wintonline' booklet.
- ★—See 'Antonbus' booklet.
- ▲—See 'Wiltsway' booklets.

EVERY CARE has been taken in compiling this index, but the Company cannot be held liable for any delay or inconvenience arising from inaccuracies, alterations to services, or any other cause.

Place	Service
ALLBROOK	40, 41, 44
ALRESFORD■...	*AV214*
ALTON	*AV214*
AMPFIELD	66
ANDOVER★	X12
BARTON STACEY■	X12
BASSETT X12, 45, 45A, 46, 46A, 47, 62, *AV214*	
BISHOPSTOKE.. .X14, 42, 42A, 43, 48, 48A, 53, 53A	
BISHOP'S WALTHAM● ... 53, 53A‡, 69, 69A	
BOYATT WOOD ... ... .40, 41, 44, 46	
CHANDLER'S FORD... 40, 41, 42, 42A, 43, 45, 45A, 46A, 47	
CHILWORTH	62
COLDEN COMMON 44, 48, 69, 69A	
COMPTON■ X12, 47, *AV214*	
CROWD HILL... ... ... .48, 69	
DURLEY● ... ... 53, 53A‡	
EASTLEIGH to	
Bishop's Waltham ... ... 53, 53A‡	
Chandler's Ford 40, 41, 42, 42A, 43	
Colden Common 44, 48	
Fair Oak X14, 48, 48A, 53, 53A	
Hedge End	49
Hiltingbury 40, 41, 42, 42A	
Horton Heath . ... 53, 53A‡	
Hypermarket... ... ...46, 53A, 65	
Marwell Zoo ... ... 48‡	
Moorgreen	49
North Baddesley	65
North Stoneham ... 48, 48A, 53, 53A, 65	
Romsey	65
Southampton (Direct) X14, 46, 48, 48A, 53	
Southampton (Indirect)	49
Southampton Airport ...X14, 49	
Stoke Common ... ... .42, 42A	
Stoke Wood... ... 43, 48, 48A, 53, 53A	
Swaythling X14, 48, 48A, 49, 53	
West End	49
Winchester 44, 48	
Woolston	49
FISHERS POND ... ... .48, 69, 69A	
FAIR OAK X14, 48, 48A, 53, 53A, 69	
FAREHAM□ 69, 69A	
FARNHAM *AV214*	
GUILDFORD *AV214*	
HEDGE END●	49
HILTINGBURY 40, 41, 42, 42A, 45, 46A‡, 66	
HORTON HEATH● ... ... 53, 53A‡	
HURSLEY ... ... .45A, 66	
HYPERMARKET 45, 45A, 46, 46A, 47, 53A, 65	
LONGPARISH★ X12	

Place	Service
LOWER UPHAM ... ... .69, 69A	
MARWELL ZOO ... .48‡, 69‡, 69A	
MOORGREEN●	49
NEWTOWN● ... ... 53, 53A‡, 69, 69A	
NORTH BADDESLEY♥ ... ,... ...62, 65	
NORTH STONEHAM... 48, 48A, 53, 53A, 65	
OAKMOUNT ESTATE.. ...42A, 43, 46A	
OTTERBOURNE ... 40, 41, 46A‡, 47	
PORTSWOOD... ... X14, 48, 48A, 53	
PYLEHILL 48A, 53A	
ROMSEY♥ 62, 65, 66	
ST. CROSS■ X12, 44, 47, 48, 69, 69A, *AV214*	
SALISBURY▲ 66	
SCRAGG HILL♥ 62, 65	
SOUTHAMPTON to●♥	
Alresford *AV214*	
Alton *AV214*	
Andover X12	
Barton Stacey. X12	
Bishop's Waltham 53	
Chandler's Ford ... 45, 45A, 46A, 47	
Colden Common 48	
Compton X12, 47, *AV214*	
Eastleigh (Direct) ... X14, 46, 48, 48A, 53	
Eastleigh (Indirect)... 49	
Fair Oak X14, 48, 48A, 53	
Farnham *AV214*	
Guildford *AV214*	
Hiltingbury ... ... 45, 46A‡	
Horton Heath 53	
Hursley 45A	
Marwell Zoo... ... ... 48‡	
Otterbourne 47	
Southampton Airport ...X14, 49	
Sutton Scotney X12	
Winchester ... X12, 47, 48, *AV214*	
SOUTHAMPTON AIRPORT X14, 49	
STOKE COMMON 42, 42A	
STOKE WOOD .. 43, 48, 48A, 53, 53A	
SUTTON SCOTNEY■.. ... ... X12	
SWANMORE● 53, 69, 69A	
SWAYTHLING... X14, 48, 48A, 49, 53	
TWYFORD■ 44, 48, 69, 69A	
VELMORE ESTATE ... 42A, 45A‡, 46	
WEST END● 49	
WHITEPARISH▲ 66	
WICKHAM□ 69, 69A	
WINCHESTER■. X12, 44, 47, 48, 66, 69, 69A, *AV214*	
WOOLSTON● 49	
WORTHY DOWN■ X12	

2

9. Write down the other places these buses will call at:
   a) Eastleigh to Woolston
   b) Southampton to Bishop's Waltham
10. Which two towns are served by most buses in this index?

24 Using a bus timetable

Look at the bus timetable for service 44:

EASTLEIGH · WINCHESTER via Boyatt Wood, Allbrook, Colden Common and Twyford — Service 44

ROUTE: 44 From Eastleigh via Twyford Rd., Shakespeare Rd., Woodside Ave., Allbrook Hill, Brambridge Rd., Church Lane, Tees Farm Rd., **Colden Common**, Spring Lane, A333, **Twyford**, Searles Hill, Twyford Rd., Saint Cross Rd. and Southgate St. **to Winchester.**

Including buses on Services 40/41 running between Eastleigh and Hiltingbury via Boyatt Wood.

Mondays to Saturdays

	NS 44	44	NS 44	NS 69	S 44	41	44	41	44	41	44	N3 41	S 41	NS 41	44	44	44	44	44
EASTLEIGH (Bus Station) ⇌	0617	0717	0752	....	0817	0932	1032	1132	1232	1332	1432	1502	1532	1602	1632	1732	1832	2132	2232
Shakespeare Road (Arrow Inn)	0621	0721	0756	....	0821	0936	1036	1136	1236	1336	1436	1506	1536	1606	1636	1736	1836	2136	2236
Boyatt Wood (Bosville North)	0624	0724	0759	....	0824	0939	1039	1139	1239	1339	1439	1509	1539	1609	1639	1739	1839	2139	2239
Allbrook (Post Office)	0626	0726	0801	....	0826	0941	1041	1141	1241	1341	1441	1511	1541	1611	1641	1741	1841	2141	2241
Hiltingbury (Ashdown Road)	♥					0952		1152		1352		1522	1552	1622	♥	♥	♥		♥
Colden Common (Spring Lane/A333)	0634	0734	0809▸	0819†	0834		1049		1249		1449				1649	1749	1849	2149	2249
Twyford (Post Office)		0738		0823	0838		1053		1253		1453				1653			2153	
St Cross (Bell Inn)		0745		0830	0845		1100		1300		1500				1700			2200	
WINCHESTER (Bus Station) ⇌		0755		0840	0855		1110		1310		1510				1710			2210	

	NS 44	NS 44	44	44	40	44	40	44	40	44	40	44	44	44
WINCHESTER (Bus Station) ⇌				0920		1120		1320		1520		1720		
St Cross (Bell Inn)				0930		1130		1330		1530		1730		
Twyford (Post Office)				0937		1137		1337		1537		1737		
Colden Common (Spring Lane/A333)	0636	0726	0822	0941		1141		1341		1541		1741	1851	2251
Hiltingbury (Ashdown Road)					1038		1238		1438		1638			
Allbrook (Post Office)	0644	0734	0830	0949	1049	1149	1249	1349	1449	1549	1649	1749	1859	2259
Boyatt Wood (Bosville North)	0646	0736	0832	0951	1051	1151	1251	1351	1451	1551	1651	1751	1901	2301
Shakespeare Road (Arrow Inn)	0649	0739	0835	0954	1054	1154	1254	1354	1454	1554	1654	1754	1904	2304
EASTLEIGH (Bus Station) ⇌	0653	0743	0839●	0958	1058	1158	1258	1358	1458	1558	1658	1758	1908	2308

Sundays

	44	44	44	44			44	44	44	44
EASTLEIGH (Bus Station) ⇌	1055	1255	1555	1755	COLDEN COMMON (Spring Lane/A333)		1111	1311	1611	1811
Shakespeare Road (Arrow Inn)	1059	1259	1559	1759	Allbrook (Post Office)		1117	1317	1617	1817
Boyatt Wood (Bosville North)	1101	1301	1601	1801	Boyatt Wood (Bosville North)		1119	1319	1619	1819
Allbrook (Post Office)	1103	1303	1603	1803	Shakespeare Road (Arrow Inn)		1121	1321	1621	1821
COLDEN COMMON (Spring Lane/A333)	1109♥	1309♥	1609♥	1809♥	EASTLEIGH (Bus Station) ⇌		1125	1325	1625	1825

SH/29.3.82 (Ad.)

CODE
S—Sats only.
NS—Not Sats.
♥—In Colden Common runs via Upper Moors Rd., New Rd. and A333 to Spring Lane.
●—On schooldays continues at 0843 to Toynbee School, arrive 0850.
▸—Change to connecting bus.
†—Time at Parish Hall, not Spring Lane/A333.
⇌—Rail Station nearby.

1. Look at the ROUTE listed at the top of the timetable and write down the next stop after:
   a) Woodside Avenue
   b) Colden Common
   c) Twyford Road
2. What does NS mean?
3. What does S mean?
4. a) What time does the first bus leave Eastleigh?
   b) What time does the first bus leave Winchester?
   c) What time does the first bus from Eastleigh to Winchester leave?
   d) What time does the last bus leave Eastleigh?
   e) Where does it finish its journey?
   f) At what time does it arrive there?
   g) How long does its journey take?
   h) What time does the last bus leave Winchester?

5. If you want to get to Winchester by 0855:
   a) What number bus do you catch?
   b) What time does it leave Allbrook?
6. Where do the service 41 buses end their journeys?
7. a) How many number 44 buses go from Winchester to Eastleigh each day?
   b) How often do they go?
8. What is the latest time you could catch a bus from Colden Common to Eastleigh?
9. If you were in Winchester and wanted to get to Twyford by lunch-time, what time would you catch the bus?
10. How long does the journey from Eastleigh to Winchester take?

25 Planning a bus journey

Use the service 44 timetable shown in the last exercise to plan the following journey:

Leave home on the first bus to Hiltingbury from Eastleigh to visit your cousin. After spending about a couple of hours there, return to Eastleigh on the next bus. Have lunch there and then catch the next bus to Winchester to do some shopping. After two hours, catch the next bus back to Eastleigh.

Copy the chart below into your book and record your journey on it.

Route Planner

From	Bus number	Leave at	To	Arrive at
Eastleigh				

26 Telephone charges

British Telecom give details of the cost of telephone calls in a leaflet called 'Telephone Charges'. Here is a section from it:

Charges for Inland Calls from 1 May 1982

Call Charge Letter*	Type of Call	Charge Rate	Time allowed for charge unit of 4.3p excl VAT (plus 0.645p VAT) on any one call	Approximate cost (including VAT) of a call of 1 min to 5 mins or 10 mins duration (see note 1)					
				1 min	2 mins	3 mins	4 mins	5 mins	10 mins
L	**Local Calls**	**Cheap**	**8 mins**	**5p**	**5p**	**5p**	**5p**	**5p**	**10p**
		Standard	2 mins	5p	5p	10p	10p	15p	25p
		Peak	1 min 30 secs	5p	10p	10p	15p	20p	35p
a	**Calls up to 56 km (35 miles)**	**Cheap**	**144 secs**	**5p**	**5p**	**10p**	**10p**	**15p**	**25p**
		Standard	45 secs	10p	15p	20p	30p	35p	69p
		Peak	30 secs	10p	20p	30p	40p	49p	99p
b	**Calls over 56 km (35 miles) and to the Channel Islands**	**Cheap**	**48 secs**	**10p**	**15p**	**20p**	**25p**	**35p**	**64p**
		Standard	16 secs	20p	40p	59p	74p	94p	£1.88
		Peak	12 secs	25p	49p	74p	99p	£1.24	£2.47
b1	**Calls over 56 km (35 miles) connected over "Low Cost Routes"***	**Cheap**	**60 secs**	**5p**	**10p**	**15p**	**20p**	**25p**	**49p**
		Standard	20 secs	15p	30p	45p	59p	74p	£1.48
		Peak	15 secs	20p	40p	59p	79p	99p	£1.98
	Calls to the Irish Republic (from Great Britain and Isle of Man)	**Cheap**	**15 secs**	**20p**	**40p**	**59p**	**79p**	**99p**	**£1.98**
		Standard	8 secs	40p	74p	£1.14	£1.48	£1.88	£3.71
		Peak	8 secs	40p	74p	£1.14	£1.48	£1.88	£3.71

	Mon	Tues	Wed	Thur	Fri	Sat	Sun
8.00am–9.00am	**Standard rate**						
9.00am–1.00pm	**Peak rate**						
1.00pm–6.00pm	**Standard rate**						
6.00pm–8.00am	**Cheap rate**						

1. How many different types of call ('charge bands') are listed?
2. a) How many charge rates are there for each charge band?
   b) What are they called?
3. a) Which is the most expensive charge rate?
   b) Which is the least expensive?
4. What do these call charge letters mean?
   L?   a?   b?

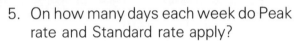

5. On how many days each week do Peak rate and Standard rate apply?
6. How many hours each day are charged at:
   a) Peak rate?
   b) Standard rate?
   c) Cheap rate?
7. On which days are calls charged at only one rate? Which rate is it?
8. How much do these calls cost?

Cheap rate
a) Local – 5 minutes
b) Local – 10 minutes
c) Up to 56 km – 5 minutes
d) Over 56 km – 3 minutes
e) Irish Republic – 1 minute

Standard rate
f) Local – 10 minutes
g) Over 56 km – 2 minutes
h) Up to 35 miles – 5 minutes
i) Local – 5 minutes

Peak rate
j) Over 35 miles – 2 minutes
k) Local – 5 minutes
l) Over 56 km on a 'low cost route' – 10 minutes

27 Using a dialling codes booklet

Each town and village in the UK has its own 'dialling code'. To dial someone in another town you use the dialling code first, then the telephone number. The dialling code booklet, produced by British Telecom, also tells you the **call charge** for each town listed.

Here is part of a dialling codes booklet:

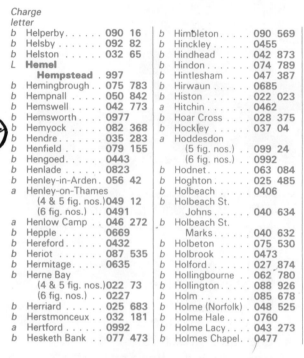

Charge letter

b	Helperby	090 16	b	Himbleton	090 569
b	Helsby	092 82	b	Hinckley	0455
b	Helston	032 65	b	Hindhead	042 873
L	**Hemel**		b	Hindon	074 789
	Hempstead	. 997	b	Hintlesham	047 387
b	Hemingbrough	075 783	b	Hirwaun	0685
b	Hempnall	050 842	b	Histon	022 023
b	Hemswell	042 773	a	Hitchin	0462
b	Hemsworth	0977	b	Hoar Cross	028 375
b	Hemyock	082 368	b	Hockley	037 04
b	Hendre	035 283	a	Hoddesdon	
b	Henfield	079 155		(5 fig. nos.)	099 24
b	Hengoed	0443		(6 fig. nos.)	0992
b	Henlade	0823	b	Hodnet	063 084
b	Henley-in-Arden	056 42	b	Hoghton	025 485
a	Henley-on-Thames		b	Holbeach	0406
	(4 & 5 fig. nos.)	049 12	b	Holbeach St.	
	(6 fig. nos.)	0491		Johns	040 634
a	Henlow Camp	046 272	b	Holbeach St.	
b	Hepple	0669		Marks	040 632
b	Hereford	0432	b	Holbeton	075 530
b	Heriot	087 535	b	Holbrook	0473
b	Hermitage	0635	b	Holford	027 874
b	Herne Bay		b	Hollingbourne	062 780
	(4 & 5 fig. nos.)	022 73	b	Hollington	088 926
	(6 fig. nos.)	0227	b	Holm	085 678
b	Herriard	025 683	b	Holme (Norfolk)	048 525
b	Herstmonceux	032 181	b	Holme Hale	0760
a	Hertford	0992	b	Holme Lacy	043 273
b	Hesketh Bank	077 473	b	Holmes Chapel	0477

Use the information shown above and on the telephone charges sheet to answer these questions:

1. How are the towns listed in the dialling codes booklet?
2. Why is Hemel Hempstead written in heavy type?
3. Write down the dialling codes for these places:
   a) Hepple
   b) Holbrook
   c) Heriot
   d) Hinckley
   e) Holme Hale
   f) Helsby
   g) Henlade
   h) Hockley
   i) Hemsworth
   j) Hitchin
4. Which places have more than one dialling code?
5. Which places have these dialling codes?
   a) 027 874
   b) 042 873
   c) 0992
   d) 035 283
   e) 088 926

Skimming Practice!

6. If these towns were added to the list, which town would they come after?
   a) Hemwell
   b) Hepstone
   c) Hoadington
   d) Hintleborough
   e) Helstanton
7. How much would these telephone calls cost?
   a) A 5-minute call to Histon at 2.00 p.m. on Thursday.
   b) A 2-minute call to Henfield at 11.00 a.m. on Monday.
   c) A 10-minute call to Hemel Hempstead at 6.30 p.m. on Wednesday.
   d) A 1-minute call to Hollingbourne at 8.30 a.m. on Tuesday.
   e) A 3-minute call to Hitchin at 9.30 a.m. on Friday.
   f) A 5-minute call to Helston at 11.00 a.m. on Saturday.
   g) A 4-minute call to Hertford at 7.30 a.m. on Monday.
   h) A 10-minute call to Holme Lacy at 12.30 p.m. on Wednesday.
   i) A 5-minute call to Hemel Hempstead at 10.30 a.m. on Friday.
   j) A 2-minute call to Henlow Camp at 10.30 a.m. on Saturday.
8. Look in your own local dialling codes booklet. What is the code for Hemel Hempstead?

28 Using the 24-hour clock

Do you know how to work out times written in the 24-hour way? If you do, have a go at writing these times in the normal way like this:

0715 ——→ 7.15 a.m.

1230 ——→ 12.30 p.m.

1400 ——→ 2.00 p.m.

1730 ——→ 5.30 p.m.

(a.m. = morning   p.m. = afternoon)

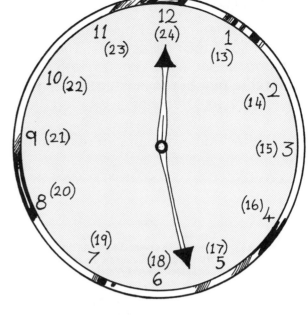

1. 1500
2. 1600
3. 1430
4. 1630
5. 1800
6. 0340
7. 1030
8. 0600
9. 1845
10. 2220

Now write these times in the 24-hour way – but watch the a.m. and p.m. signs!

6.30 p.m. ——→ 1830

6.30 a.m. ——→ 0630

11. 5.00 a.m.
12. 5.00 p.m.
13. 2.30 p.m.
14. 1.00 a.m.
15. 7.40 p.m.
16. 7.30 a.m.
17. 1.55 p.m.
18. 9.05 a.m.
19. 11.30 p.m.
20. 4.15 p.m.

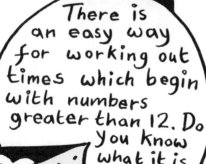

There is an easy way for working out times which begin with numbers greater than 12. Do you know what it is?

BRAIN BOX

29 Railway routes

Inside their timetables British Rail show a route map of their rail services. The numbers beside each route tell you which **timetable number** to look up (trains don't have numbers like buses).

Look at this route map of part of Southern Region's rail network:

3. Which stations are served by
   a) a local service only?
   b) a rush-hour service only?

4. What do you think the 'wavy line' symbol between Portsmouth and Ryde stands for?

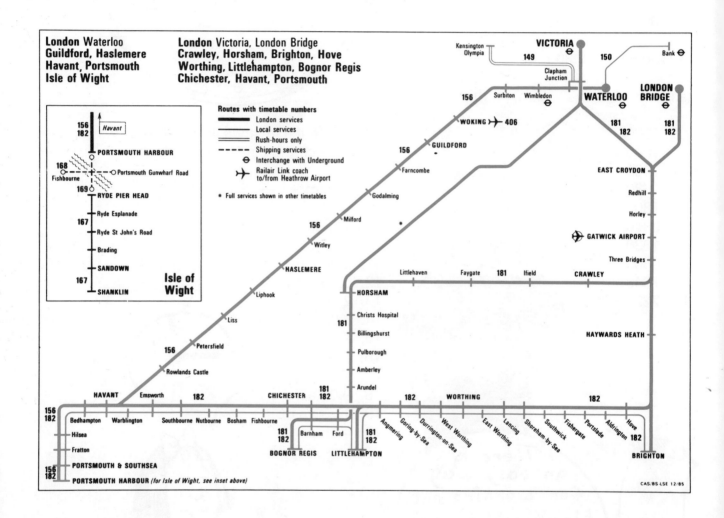

1. Write down the number of the timetable you would look up to find these services:
   a) Haslemere to Guildford
   b) Crawley to Horsham
   c) Havant to Chichester
   d) Waterloo to Bank
   e) Fratton to Portsmouth Harbour
   .f) Sandown to Shanklin
2. Which timetable shows the Railair Link to Heathrow Airport?

There is also an index to all the stations shown in the timetables. On the page opposite you will see part of it. Now answer questions 5 to 12.

5. In which timetables will you find these stations?
   a) Beccles
   b) Ballater
   c) Basildon
   d) Aspley Guise

e) Battle
f) Avonmouth
g) Beaulieu Road
h) Southampton

6. Which town in the index has the largest number of train services?

7. Could you park your car at Baldock station?

8. Could you get something to eat at Aylesbury station? How do you know?

9. Which stations have facilities for disabled people?

10. Could you hire a car from these stations? Write YES or NO.
a) Bath Spa
b) Aylesbury

Notes of facilities:
Catering   — Travellers-Fare or equivalent
Disabled   — Disabled 'core' station (see page 3)
Parcels   — Rail Express Parcels/Red Star
Rail Drive   — Godfrey Davis self-drive car hire
Trolleys   — Passenger self-help trolleys
Underground — Station also served by London Regional Transport
★   — Indicates that facility is available

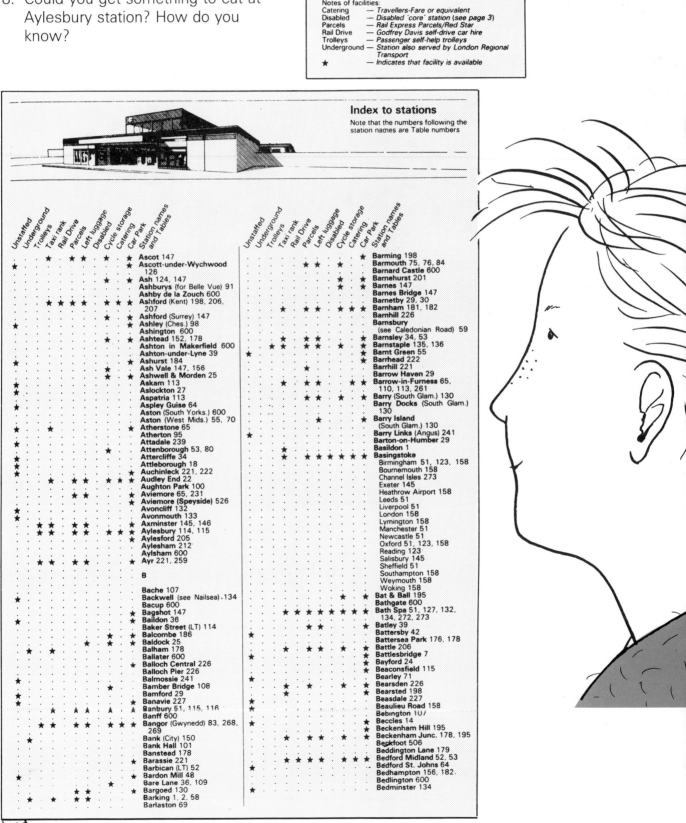

39

c) Bedford Midland
d) Bangor
e) Axminster

11. Which stations are served by the London Underground?

12. Which station would you find in timetable 24?

30 Using a railway timetable

Table 158 in the railway timetable gives details of services from London Waterloo to Bournemouth and also the return journey. Because there are so many trains on these services the timetable lasts for about twenty-three pages!

Here are two of those pages, showing part of the Saturday train services:

Table 158
London, Basingstoke and Southampton to Bournemouth

Saturdays
Throughout

		J			J	E		A			J		D		C		E		J	A
London Waterloo ⊖ ....152, 156 d		05 45			06 12	06 45	06 50		07 12		07 45	07 42	08 12	08 35		08 45		08 42	09 10	09 12	09 35
Surbiton ....152, 156 d		05 39			06 28	06 39			07 28		07 37	07 50	08 28			08 37		08 58	09 07	09 28	
406 Heathrow Airport ⇐ ....d																08 10					
Woking .. .. .. 156 d		06 10			06 43	07 10	07 17		07 43		08 10	08 13	08 43			09 10		09 13	09 36	09 43	
Brookwood .. .. 156 d		06 48				07 48				08 18	08 48	09 15					09 18		09 48	
Farnborough (Main) .. .. d		06 55				07 55				08 25	08 55						09 25		09 55	
Fleet .. .. .. d		07 00				08 00				08 30	09 05						09 30		10 00	
Winchfield .. .. d		07 05				08 05				08 35	09 05						09 35		10 05	
Hook .. .. .. d		07 08				08 08				08 38	09 08						09 38		10 08	
Basingstoke .. .. d		06 32	07 02	07a15	07 32	07a38	07 45	08a15	08 23	08 32	08b48	09a15		09 28	09 32	09 45	09b48	09a57	10a15	10 23
Micheldever .. ⇐ d			07 12					07 55			08 58						09 58			
Winchester .. .. d		06 49	07 21	➡	07 49		08 04		08 43	08 49	09 07			09 46	09 49	10 04	10 07			10 43
Shawford .. .. d			07 26				08 09				09 12						10 12			
Eastleigh .. .. d		06 45	06 58	07 32		07 58	08 14		08a52	08 58	09 17			09 55	09 58		10 19			10a52
Southampton Airport .. d		07 02		07 35		08 02	08 18		09 02	09 21						10 02				
Swaythling .. .. d	06 49			07 38			08 20			09 23							10 23			
St. Denys .. .. 165 d	06 52		⟵	07 41			08 23			09 26							10 26			
Southampton .. .. 165 a	06 57	07 10	06 57	07 46		08 10	08 29		09 10	09 32		09 45	09 32	10 04	10 10	10 25	10 34		10 45	
Southampton .. .. 165 d	07 15	07 14	07 15	07 47		08 13		08 47		09 13	09 48		09 45	09 48	10 05	10 13	10 26	10 48		10 45
Millbrook (Hants) .. .. d			07 18	07 49				08 49						09 50						
Redbridge .. .. 165 d			07 21	07 52				08 52						09 53						
Totton .. .. .. d			07 23	07 54				08 54						09 55						
Lyndhurst Road .. .. d			07 27	07 59				08 59						10 00						
Beaulieu Road .. .. d			07 31	08 03				09 03						10 04						
Brockenhurst .. .. a		07 29	07 38	08 09		08 28		09 09		09 28				10 10	10 19	10 28				
160 Lymington Town .. .. a		07 49				08 49		09p19		09 49				10p19	10 49					
160 Lymington Pier .. .. a		07 51				08 51		09p21		09 51				10p21	10 51					
Yarmouth Slipway .. Ship a		08 30				09 30		10x00		10 30				11p00	11 30					
Brockenhurst .. .. d		07 29		08 10		08 28		09 10		09 28				10 10	10 19	10 28				
Sway .. .. .. d				08 15				09 15						10 15						
New Milton .. .. d		07 36		08 20		08 36		09 20		09 36				10 20	10 27	10 36				
Hinton Admiral .. .. d				08 24				09 24						10 24						
Christchurch .. .. d		07 44		08 29		08 44		09 29		09 44				10 29	10 35	10 44				
Pokesdown .. .. d				08 32				09 32						10 32						
Bournemouth .. .. a		07 51		08 36		08 51		09 36		09 51				10 13	10 36	10 41	10 51	11 00		11 13

		H		K		G		D	D	J			B		L	E		J		A
London Waterloo ⊖ ....152, 156 d		09 40	09 45	10 00	09 42	10 10	10 12	10 14	10 26	10 35			10 45		10 42	11 10	11 12	11 35		
Surbiton ....152, 156 d			09 37	09 58	09 58	10 07	10 28						10 37		10 58		11 07	11 28		
406 Heathrow Airport ⇐ ....d			09 10										10 10		10n40					
Woking .. .. .. 156 d			10 10	10a26	10 13	10 38	10 43	10u51					11 10		11 13	11 36	11 43			
Brookwood .. .. 156 d			10 18		10 48										11 25		11 48			
Farnborough (Main) .. .. d			10 25		10 55										11 30		11 55			
Fleet .. .. .. d			10 30		11 00										11 30		12 00			
Winchfield .. .. d			10 35		11 05										11 35		12 05			
Hook .. .. .. d			10 38		11 09										11 38		12 08			
Basingstoke .. .. d		10 30	10 32		10b48	11a00	11a16						11 32	11r51	11b48	12a08	11a57	12a16		12 22
Micheldever .. .. d					10 58								11 58							
Winchester .. .. d		10 49			11 07								11 49	12r11	12 07					12 42
Shawford .. .. d					11 12								12 12							
Eastleigh .. .. d		10 58			11 19								11 58		12 19					12a52
Southampton Airport .. d		11 02											12 02							
Swaythling .. .. d					11 23										12 23					
St. Denys .. .. 165 d					11 26										12 26					
Southampton .. .. 165 a		10 34	11r01	11 10	11r29	11r34		11r30		11 45	11r34	12 10	12r30	12 32	12r38		12 45	12 32		
Southampton .. .. 165 d		10 48	11r02	11 13	11r22	11 48		11r31		11 45	11r34	12 13	12r31	12 48	12r40		12 45	12 48		
Millbrook (Hants) .. .. d		10 50										11 50						12 50		
Redbridge .. .. 165 d		10 53										11 53						12 53		
Totton .. .. .. d		10 55										11 55						12 55		
Lyndhurst Road .. .. d		11 00										12 00						13 00		
Beaulieu Road .. .. d		11 04										12 04						13 04		
Brockenhurst .. .. a		11 10		11 28	11 37					12 10	12 28						13 10			
160 Lymington Town .. .. a		11p22		11q49	11 49					12p26	12 49						13p19			
160 Lymington Pier .. .. a				11q51	11 53						12 51						13p21			
Yarmouth Slipway .. Ship a				12q30	12 30						13 30						14p00			
Brockenhurst .. .. d		11t11		11 28						12 10	12 28						13v10			
Sway .. .. .. d		11t15								12 15							13v15			
New Milton .. .. d		11t20		11 36						12 20	12 36						13v20			
Hinton Admiral .. .. d		11t24								12 24							13v24			
Christchurch .. .. d		11t29		11 44						12 29	12 44						13v29			
Pokesdown .. .. d		11t32								12 32							13v32			
Bournemouth .. .. a		11t36	11 30	11 51				12 00	12 05	12 13	12 36	12 51	13 00		13 08		13 13	13v36		

For general notes see front of book

A From Reading (Table 123) to Portsmouth Harbour (Table 165)
B 28 May and 25 June to 24 September from Wolverhampton dep. 08 49. From 8 October from Liverpool Lime Street dep. 07 20 to Poole (Table 51)
C From Derby dep. 06 00 to Poole (Table 51)
D 23 July to 3 September
E To Exeter St. David's (Table 145)
G To Salisbury (Table 145)
H 28 May to 24 September
J To Weymouth (Table 159)
K Until 3 September
L Until 1 October. From Liverpool Lime Street dep. 07 50 to Poole (Table 51)

b Arr. 3 minutes earlier
n Until 1 October
p Until 3 September
q From 10 September
r Until 3 September arr. 11 47. Passengers can arrive Southampton 11 36 by changing at St. Denys
t Until 29 October 6 minutes later
v Until 1 October 4 minutes later
z Until 1 October arr. 13 46

729

1. On which pages will these two timetables be found?
2.
   a) What time does the first train leave Waterloo?
   b) What time does it arrive in Bournemouth?
   c) How long does the journey take?
   d) What time does the train stop in Eastleigh?
   e) What time does it arrive in Southampton?
   f) How long does the journey from Eastleigh to Southampton take?
3.
   a) What time does the first stopping train ('slow' train) from Basingstoke to Bournemouth leave?
   b) What time does it arrive in Bournemouth?

Table 158
Bournemouth to Southampton, Basingstoke and London

Saturdays — From 21 January

		K						G	B	J	H	E
Bournemouth	d	00 01				05 54	06 18		06 50 06 54 07 15 07 41			
Pokesdown	d						06 22		06 58 07 18			
Christchurch	d	00 10				06 00	06 26		07 02 07 23			
Hinton Admiral	d					06 05			07 07 07 27			
New Milton	d	00 19				06 11	06 33		07 12 07 31			
Sway	d					06 16			07 18 07 35			
Brockenhurst	d	00 27				06 20	06 40		07 07 07 22 07 40			
Yarmouth Slipway Ship	d											06k40
160 Lymington Pier	d						06 26		06 55			07 58
160 Lymington Town	d						06 26		06 57			08 00
Brockenhurst	d	00 33				06 21	06 41		07 23 07 41			08b11
Beaulieu Road	d					06 29			07 47			08 17
Lyndhurst Road	d					06 34			07 51			08 21
Totton	d					06 36			07 57			08 25
Redbridge 165	d					06 39			07 59			08 28
Millbrook (Hants) 165	d					06 42			08 03			08 31
Southampton 165	a	00 49				06 42	06 56		07 26 07 37 08 05 08 09		08 05	08 34
Southampton 165	d	01 20 05 19		05 46 06 03	06 43	06 56	07 13 07 27 07 39 08 13 08 09			08 13	08 35
St. Denys 165	d		05a28 05 37	05a55 06a12 06 17 06 51		07 17				08 17	08 41
Swaythling	d		05 40	06 20 06 54		07 21				08 21	08 44
Southampton Airport	d			06 56		07 47					
Eastleigh	d	01 40	05 45	06 25 07a00	07 07	07 26 07 52				08 26	08a48
Shawford	d		05 50	06 30		07 31				08 31	
Winchester	d	01e54	05a55	06 35	07 16	07 36 08 01				08 45	
Micheldever	d			06 44		07 45					
Basingstoke	d	02a12 02e31	05 56 06 26	06 56	07 26 07 34 07 50 07 56 08a01 08 19			08 26 08 39	09 01	
Hook	d		06 02 06 32	07 02	07 32	08 06		08 32	09 02	
Winchfield	d		06 06 06 36	07 06	07 36	08 06		08 36	09 06	
Fleet	d		06 14 06 44	07 14	07 44	08 14		08 44	09 14	
Farnborough (Main)	d		06 18 06 48	07 18	07 48	08 18		08 48	09 18	
Brookwood 156	d		06 25 06 55	07 25	07 55	08 25		08 55	09 25	
Woking 156	a	02 54	06 31 07 01	07 31	08 01	08 10 08 31	08 39	09 01 09 01 09 31 09 21		
406 Heathrow Airport	a				08 55		09 55		09 55		
Surbiton 152, 156	a	03 20	06 45 07 15	07 45	08 15	08 38 08 45	09 08	09 15 09 38 09 45		
London Waterloo 152, 156	a	03 45	07 03 07 31	08 01	08 31 08 17 08 38 09 01	09 04	09 18 09 31 09 28 10 01 09 48		

		J		G		A	C			J		D	
Bournemouth	d	08 02 08 12 08 41				09 00		09 12 09 41		09 53	10 00	
Pokesdown	d	08 15						09 15			10 06	
Christchurch	d	08 08 08 19				09 06		09 19			10 06	
Hinton Admiral	d	08 24						09 24			10 13	
New Milton	d	08 15 08 28				09 13		09 28			10 13	
Sway	d	08 33						09 33				
Brockenhurst	a	08 22 08 38				09 20		09 38			10 20	
Yarmouth Slipway Ship	d					08 10					09 10	
160 Lymington Pier	d					08 58					09 58	
160 Lymington Town	d					09 00					10 00	
Brockenhurst	d	08 23 08 39				09 21		09 39			10 21	
Beaulieu Road	d	08 45						09 45				
Lyndhurst Road	d	08 49						09 49				
Totton	d	08 53						09 53				
Redbridge 165	d	08 55						09 55				
Millbrook (Hants)	d	08 59						09 59				
Southampton 165	a	08 37 09 01 09 09		09 01		09 35		10 01	10 09	10 01 10 25	10 35	
Southampton 165	d	08 39 09 13 09 09		09 13		09 37		10 13	10 09	10 13 10 27	10 37	
St. Denys	d			09 17						10 17		
Swaythling	d			09 21						10 21		
Southampton Airport	d	08 48		09 23		09 46					10 46	
Eastleigh	d	08 52		09 26	09 43 09 52			10 26		10 52	
Shawford	d			09 31					10 31			
Winchester	d	09 01		09 36	09 53 10 01			10 36 10 45		11 01	
Micheldever	d			09 45				10 45			
Basingstoke	d	09 19		09 26 09 29 09 56	10a15 10 16 10 19			10 26 10 56 11a06	11 19	
Hook	d			09 32 10 02				11 02		
Winchfield	d			09 36 10 06				11 06		
Fleet	d			09 44 10 14				11 14		
Farnborough (Main)	d			09 48 10 18				11 18		
Brookwood 156	d			09 55 10 25				11 25		
Woking 156	a	09 39		10 01 09 53 10 31		10 36 10 39		11 01	11 39	
406 Heathrow Airport	a	10 55				11 55		11 55		12 55	
Surbiton 152, 156	a	10 08		10 15 10 15 10 45		11 08		11 15	11 45	12 08	
London Waterloo 152, 156	a	10 04		10 18 10 31 10 21 11 01		11 03 11 05		11 18 11 31	12 01	12 04	

For general notes see front of book

A From Portsmouth Harbour (Table 165) to Reading (Table 123)
B From Poole dep. 06 38 to Liverpool Lime Street (Table 51)
C From Newton Abbot dep. 06 48 (Table 145)
D From Poole dep. 09 40 to Newcastle and Leeds (Table 51)
E From Exeter St. David's (Table 145)
G From Salisbury (Table 145)
H From Yeovil Junction dep. 06 50 (Table 145)
J From Weymouth (Table 159)
K From Weymouth. Limited accommodation (Table 159)
L Stops at Wimbledon 06 57

b Arr. 3 minutes earlier
e Arr. 5 minutes earlier
k From 7 April

741

c) How long does the journey take?

d) How much longer does it take than the earlier 'fast' train?

4. a) Which London–Bournemouth express is faster, the 1014 or the 1026?

   b) How long does it take to complete its journey?

   c) How much faster is this than the 0545 from Waterloo?

5. a) What time does the first train from Bournemouth leave?

   b) Where is its destination?

   c) What time does it arrive there?

   d) How long does the journey take?

   e) Why does it take so long?

6. If you wanted to get to Heathrow Airport by 10 o'clock, what train would you catch from Bournemouth?

7. What time does the first train with a buffet car leave Bournemouth?

8. Where has the train which leaves Bournemouth at 0841 just come from?

9. The Waterloo–Bournemouth express arrives in Bournemouth at 12.00. What time did it leave Waterloo and what was its last stop before Bournemouth?

10. A train arrives in Bournemouth at 1100, heading for Poole. Where has it come from and what time did it set out on its journey?

11. If you were travelling from Brockenhurst to Southampton, which train would you have to catch to get home by five past ten?

12. If you wanted to get back to Eastleigh just before noon, what time would you leave Winchester?

31 Planning a train journey

If you look back at the railway network shown in exercise 30 you can find Southampton, Basingstoke, Salisbury and Romsey.

You are going to make an imaginary journey to visit some relatives and friends, using the train services shown on the map.

You already have the service 158 timetables. Opposite are the timetables for services to Salisbury and Romsey.

And here is your imaginary day excursion:

You live five minutes walk away from Southampton railway station. You are going to visit your aunt at 32, Station Road, Basingstoke on Saturday. She is expecting you to arrive just in time for coffee at 10 o'clock. After staying for lunch you are going to Salisbury in time to meet your cousin just after half past two. You are going to do some shopping and visit the cathedral, then catch a train to Romsey in time to call on a friend just after 5 o'clock. You aim to spend exactly two hours there. After tea you want to get back to Southampton in time to watch your favourite TV programme at 7.30.

1. Use all the information in the route map and timetables to copy and complete this route plan of your journey:

Route Planner
Journey date:

From	Depart	Train Service	To	Arrive
1. Southampton				
2. Coffee and lunch at aunt's house				
3.				

Table 145

London to Salisbury and Exeter

For principal services from London Paddington to Exeter see Table 135

		A		C	H				C	A					
London Waterloo ⊖ .. 158 d	23p12 01 40	..	05 45 06 50 07 45	08 37 09 10		10 10 11 10		12 10 12 10 13 10 14 10 15 10 16 10		17 10
156 Surbiton .. d	23p28		05 39 06 39 07 37	09 07		10 07 11 07		12 07 12 07 13 07 14 07 15 07 16 07		17 07
406 Heathrow Airport ✈ .. d	..	..	.. ..	08 10		09 10 10x40		11x40 11x40 12x40 13x40 14x40 15x40		16x40
Woking .. 158 d	23p43 02 10		06 10 07 17 08 10	09 36		10 38 11 36		11p53 11p53 13 25 13 53 14 53 16 14		17 36
123 Reading .. d	23p00		06 26 06 53 07 53	09 19		09 53 10e53				16 53
Basingstoke .. 158 d	00 18		07 00 07 40 08 34	09 58		11 01 11 58 12 05		13 01 13 04 13 58 15 01 15 58 17 01		17 58
Overton .. d			07 10 07 50 08 44			11 12 12 15		13 11 13 15 15 12 17 12		
Whitchurch (Hants) .. d			07 16 07 56 08 50			11 19 12 21		13 17 13 21 15 19 17 19		
Andover .. d	00 40 02 58		07 25 08 06 08 59	10 16		11 31 12 16 12 30		13 28 13 30 14 16 15 31 16 16 17 30		18 16
Grateley .. d			07 34 08 14 09 08			11 40 12 39		13 37 13 39 15 40 17 39		
Salisbury .. a	00 58 03 25		07 47 08 26 09 21	09p54 10 34		11 53 12 34 12 52		13 52 13 52 14 34 15 53 16 34 17 52		18 34
182 Brighton .. d				06p32 08 20 09 20 09 20		09 32		11 32 13 32		15 32
165 Portsmouth & Southsea .. d			07 00	08 02 10 02 10 02		11 14		13 14 15 14		17 14
165 Southampton .. d			07 52	08 55 09 55 10 53 10 53		11 55		13 55 15 55		17 54
Salisbury .. d	03 33	06 32	08 39	09 57 10 39 11 25 11 25		12 39		14 39 16 39		18 39
Tisbury .. d		06 48	08 55	10 55		12 55		14 55 16 55		18 55
Gillingham (Dorset) .. d	04b08	06 59	09 07	11 07		13 07		15 09 17 06		19 06
Sherborne .. d	04c32	07 14	09 21	10 36 11 21		13 21		15 21 17 21		19 21
Yeovil Junction .. d	04a40	07 23	09 28	10 44 11 28 12 07 12 07		13 28		15 29 17 28		19 28
Crewkerne .. d		07 33	09 38	11 38		13 38		15 38 17 38		19 38
Axminster .. d		07 50	09 54	11 08 11 54 12 30 12 36		13 54		15 54 17 54	18 33 19 54	
Honiton .. d	07 15 08 04		10 07	11 25 12 07 12 45 12 51		14 07		16 07 18 07	18h55 20 07	
Feniton .. d	07 21 08 11		10 14	12 14					19 01 20 14	
Whimple .. d	07 27 08 16		10 19						19 07	
Pinhoe .. d	07 34 08 25		10 28							
Exeter Central .. a	07 41 08 30		10 34	11 44 12 27 13 10 13 09		14 27		16 26 18 26	19 18 20 29	
Exeter St. David's .. a	07 45 08 35		10 38	11 50 12 34 13 08 13 15		14 32		16 34 18 31	19 24 20 34	
135 Paignton .. a	08c45 10a20		11g40	13 01 14A00 14 18 14 23		16 20		18m20 20 20	21 01 21v59	
135 Plymouth .. a	09c23 10a17		12g08	12 52 14 10 14 22 14 41		16 00		17n57 19u52	21 02 22 18	

Table 165

Salisbury, Southampton, Eastleigh and Fareham to Portsmouth

Saturdays

		L	A	B		B	A		Q	A		U	A		B J		V	A
Salisbury.. d	16 09		16 31 16 44		17 24		17 44		18 24		18 44		19 39 19 50		20 39		21 38	22 20
Dean .. d			16 58				17 58				18 58		20 04				21 52	22 34
Dunbridge .. d			17 04				18 04				19 04		20 10				21 58	22 40
Romsey .. d			17 09		17 44		18 09				19 09		19 59 20 16		20 59		22 03	22b48
Redbridge .. 158 d			17 17				18 17				19 17		20 24				22 11	22 56
Southampton ..158 a	16 40		17 00 17 22		17 55		18 22		18 54		19 22		20 12 20 29		21 12		22 16	23 01
	16 44		17 03 17 23		17 56		18 23		18 55		19 23		20 15 20 30		21 15 21 29		22 18	23 02
St. Denys .. 158 d			17 29				18 29				19 29		20 36		21 36		22 23	23 07
Bitterne .. d			17 32				18 32				19 32		20 38		21 38		22 26	23 10
Woolston .. d			17 36				18 36				19 36		20 42		21 42		22 30	23 14
Sholing .. d			17 38				18 38				19 38		20 45		21 45		22 32	23 16
Netley .. d			17 42				18 42				19 42		20 49		21 49		22 36	23 20
Hamble .. d			17 44				18 44				19 44		20 51		21 51		22 38	23 22
Bursledon .. d			17 48				18 48				19 48		20 54		21 54		22 42	23 26
Swanwick .. d			17 52				18 52				19 52		20 59		21 59		22 46	23 30
Eastleigh .. d			17 03				18 03				19 03		20 03		21 03		22 03	23 03
Botley .. d			17 11				18 11				19 11		20 11		21 11		22 11	23 11
Fareham .. d	17 10		17 27 22 17 28 17 59		18 20		18 25 18 59		19 21 19 26 19 59 20 20 22 20 38		21 05 21 22		21 38 22 05 22 22 22 52 23 22 23 36	
Portchester .. d			17 27		18 04		18 30 19 04		19 31 20 04 20 20		21 22		21 11 22 27 22 58 23 27 23 42	
Cosham .. d			17 32		18 09		18 29 18 35 19 09		19 30 19 36 20 09 20 32		21 15 21 32		21 46 22 15 22 32 23 23 02 23 23 46	
Hilsea 166, 182 d																	
Fratton 166, 182 a			17 40		18 17		18 42 19 17		19 43 20 17 20 40		21 23 21 40		22 22 40 23 10 23 40 23 54	
Portsmouth & Southsea 166, 182 a			17 45 17 45 18 20		18 38 18 45 19 20		19 46 20 20 43 20 20 54		21 56 22 22 43 23 13 23 57	
Portsmouth Harbour 166, 182 a			17 46 17 52 18 24		18 43 18 49 19 24		19 50		20 47 21 00 21 30 21 47		22 00 22 30 22 47 23 16 23 46 00 01	

For general notes see front of book

A From Reading (Tables 123 and 158)
B From Bristol Temple Meads (Table 132)
C From Cardiff Central (Table 132)
D Until 14 January
E From 21 January

G Until 3 September. From Cardiff Central dep. 09 50 to Weymouth (Tables 132 and 159)

H Until 25 June and from 3 September from Bristol Temple Meads dep. 11 10, 2 July to 27 August from Cardiff Central dep. 10 15 (Table 132)

J Until 1 October. From Cardiff Central (Table 132)

K From 8 October. From Cardiff Central (Table 132)

L From Penzance dep. 10 45 (Tables 145 and 182)

Q From Cardiff Central dep. 16 10, 16 15 from 8 October to Brighton

U From Westbury (Table 132)
V From Weston-super-Mare dep 19 40 (Table 132)
Y From 21 January is through train from London Waterloo dep. 02 45 (Table 158)
Z 18 June to 17 September. From Leeds dep. 22 21 (Friday) (Table 51)

b Arr. 3 minutes earlier
e Arr. 5 minutes earlier

> From time to time it is necessary to undertake extensive engineering work at weekends. This frequently affects Saturday night/Sunday services and passengers are advised to look for specific announcements of possible diversion and delays, making a final check at stations or telephone enquiry bureaux.

756

2. Can you use the railway timetables to make up a day excursion yourself?

32 Information from television

If you plan the programmes you watch, television can give you a great deal of information about all sorts of things.

It is particularly good at presenting information about things which are happening in the world today. The NEWS gives short 'headlines' and DOCUMENTARIES look at things in close detail.

When you use television for information, make notes as you watch – or you'll forget the details. Of course, a video recorder will help you to 'store' the information until you've got time to write it down. (If you haven't got one, an ordinary tape recorder will often plug into your television, so at least you can **hear** the news!)

There are now four television channels, and you need to use all of them to find the greatest amount of information.

On pages 46 and 47 are sections of *Radio Times* and *TV Times* which show some of the programmes shown on one Friday evening.

Look at the viewing information for the four TV channels, then answer these questions:

1. What time does the first programme shown on each channel begin?
    a) ITV
    b) Channel Four
    c) BBC 1
    d) BBC 2
2. What time does the last programme shown on each channel begin?
    a) ITV
    b) Channel Four
    c) BBC 1
    d) BBC 2
3. Is this a complete evening's viewing?
4. If you switched your TV on at 6.30, what four choices of programme would you have?

5. At one point in the evening, three of the TV Channels start a programme at exactly the same time. At what time do all three programmes begin and on which channels are they shown?
6. How long do these programmes last?
    a) *The Animal Express*
    b) *The Tudor Face*
    c) *Points of View*
    d) *Civilisation*
    e) *News at 5.45*
    f) *The Brides of Fu Manchu*
    g) *The Friday Alternative*
    h) *Mass Communication*
7. Write down the names of these actors, presenters or technicians:
    a) The producer of *The Dinosaur Trail*.
    b) The presenter of *Winner Takes All*.
    c) The star of *The Brides of Fu Manchu*.

d) The editor of *About Anglia*.
e) The presenter of *Friday Sportstime*.
f) The commentators in *Jack High*.
g) Captain Foster in *The Raid*.
h) The director of *Rainbow*.
i) The star of *The Coral Jungle*.
j) The newsreader on the *Nine O'Clock News*.
k) The presenter of *The Amateur Naturalist*.
l) The producer of *Points of View*.
m) The cameraman on *Ladybirds*.
n) The newsreader on *Evening News*.
o) The writer of *In Search of Paradise*.
p) The series consultant for *The Dinosaur Trail*.
q) The presenter of *Civilisation*.
r) The star of *The Animal Express*.
s) The narrator of *In Search of Paradise*.
t) The writer of *The Three Knights*.

8. What is showing on:
   a) Central TV instead of *Mr Merlin*?
   b) Yorkshire TV instead of *About Anglia*?
   c) Thames/LWT instead of *Mr Merlin*?
9. How many new series are shown?

10. What times do news programmes begin on:
    a) ITV?
    b) BBC 1?
    c) Channel Four?
    d) BBC 2?
11. Which programme would you watch if you were interested in:
    a) quiz games?
    b) underwater exploration?
    c) animals?
    d) gardening?
    e) dinosaurs?
    f) bowls?
    g) political arguments?
    h) sport?
    i) Westerns?
    j) Open University programmes?
12. Write down the programmes you would make notes from about an important event that took place abroad today.
13. Which programme would you watch to find out more about the struggle between the Conservative Party and Labour Party?
14. Which programme claims to give the news from a very different point of view?
15. Which channel has least national news at this time in the evening?

4.0 to 5.15
Children's ITV
presented by
MIKE REID

Rainbow
SINGALONG

Appearing are Geoffrey Hayes, Stanley Bates, Jane Tucker, Rod Burton, Freddy Marks and Roy Skelton. Join Geoffrey, Bungle, Zippy and George in a singalong.
WRITER GEOFFREY HAYES
RESEARCH MEGAN LANDER
DIRECTOR TERRY STEEL
PRODUCER LESLEY BURGESS
EXECUTIVE PRODUCER
CHARLES WARREN

4.20 Doris
THE BIRTHDAY PARTY
Doris is too inquisitive, so her friends keep her guessing about their birthday presents. Last in the present series.

4.25 The Animal Express
ALISON HOLLOWAY
At San Diego Zoo Polly the lion-tailed macaque gives birth.
Oracle sub-titles page 199

4.50
NEW SERIES
The Dinosaur Trail
JOHN NOAKES
Dr Beverly Halstead
Films, facts, figures and fun about dinosaurs, presented by John Noakes. Series consultant is Dr Beverly Halstead.
See page 69
RESEARCH JUDY BRAGGINS
DIRECTOR IAN WHITE
PRODUCER DIANA BRAMWELL
EXECUTIVE PRODUCER
STEPHEN LEAHY
Granada Television Production

5.15 Mr Merlin
I WAS A TEENAGE LOSER
Zac uses flashes of his apprentice-wizard magic to help Leo overcome a spell of self-doubt.

Max	Barnard Hughes
Zac	Clark Brandon
Leo	Jonathan Prince
Alex	Elaine Joyce

News at 5.45

6.0
About Anglia
GRAHAM BELL
CHRISTINE WEBBER
Switch on for the programme that's really regional. People, places, controversies and curiosities, they're all in today's edition. Gerry Harrison and Stuart Jarrold bring you news, action and comment on the region's sports. Paul Barnes presents your criticisms, comments and controversies in *Write Now*, and *Patrick's Pantry* has another helping of food, fun and Irish blarney. John Bacon presents today's news and Michael Hunt and David Brooks bring you the weekend weather.
EDITOR JIM WILSON
DIRECTORS
ALAN BURRELL, HUGH DAVIES
Anglia Television Production

7.0
Winner Takes All
JIMMY TARBUCK
Another round of the general knowledge gambling game. Question master Geoffrey Wheeler calls the odds, assisted by Mari Kirkwood and Linda Lewis. Questions set by Deborah Sutherland, additional material by Wally Malston.
CONTESTANT RESEARCH
SHIRLEY E JONES
DESIGNER
GORDON LIVESEY
PRODUCER DON CLAYTON
Yorkshire Television Production

Programmes as Anglia except:

THAMES/LWT 12.30 Home Sweet Home; 1.20 Thames News; 5.15 Young Doctors; 6.0 The 6 O'Clock Show; 10.30 Making of Modern London; 11.0 **Film — Lost Honour of Katherine Blum.** Heavy drama. German film with subtitles; 1.15 Rawhide; 2.15 Night Thoughts.

TVS 1.20 TVS News; 3.30 That's Hollywood; 5.15 Blockbusters; 6.0 Coast to Coast; 6.30 Friday Sportshow; 10.30 **Film — The Mephisto Waltz.** Sinister tale set in the world of music starring Alan Alda and Jacqueline Bisset; 12.30 Company.

CENTRAL 1.20 Central News; 1.30 **Film — Delusions of Grandeur.** Louis de Funes as adventurer Don Salluste in French comedy with English dialogue; 3.30 Sons and Daughters; 5.15 Blockbusters; 6.0 Central News and Friday Show; 10.30 Hill Street Blues; 11.30 Central News; 11.35 **Film — The Last of Sheila.** Murder mystery with Richard Benjamin, Dyan Cannon, James Mason.

YORKSHIRE 1.20 Calendar News; 3.30 Sons & Daughters; 5.15 Blockbusters; 6.0 Calendar; 10.30 Newhart; 11.0 Thriller.

##
CHANNEL FOUR

4.45
The Tudor Face
ISAAC OLIVER
Last of the series of programmes shown this week.

5.0 In Search of Paradise
MICHAEL HORDERN
THE FINAL CHALLENGE
In this, the final programme of the series, we look at the future of the garden. The trends for the future are clear: the apartment, the second home, the car, and the ever encroaching road systems have reshaped the way we live with nature. The challenge of the future is cooperate or destroy? Narrator is Sir Michael Hordern.
WRITER RENE ALLEAU
DIRECTORS
JIM HANELY, REVEL GUEST
PRODUCER REVEL GUEST
Trans Atlantic Films Production

5.30
The Abbott and Costello Show
The show that brings some of the classic comedy routines of Bud Abbott and Lou Costello to the television screen.

6.0
The Coral Jungle
LEONARD NIMOY
MYSTERIES OF THE REEF
Underwater photographers Ben and Eva Cropp continue their exploration of Australia's Great Barrier Reef, with Eva dancing an underwater ballet with a giant manta ray and feeding moray eels barehanded.

7.0
Channel Four News
With Peter Sissons, Trevor McDonald and Sarah Hogg.

Weather

7.30 The Friday Alternative
If you think television news is predictable, take a look at one provocative alternative.
Diverse Productions

8.0
The Amateur Naturalist
GERALD DURRELL
THE OTHER NEW YORKERS
Surrounded by the glass and concrete of New York City, Gerald and Lee Durrell find nature flourishing in close proximity to man. Durrell describes the dependency of mice on man in our cities. On a vacant lot in Manhattan, the Durrells construct a 'tenement forest' to attract such creatures as the zebra jumping spider, which leaps athletically on its helpless prey. For an accompanying folder send a £1.50p cheque/PO, made payable to Channel Four TV Ltd, and a sae to: The Conservation Foundation, Aviation House, 129 Kingsway, London WC2B 6NH.
DIRECTOR ALASTAIR BROWN
Dorling Kindersley Television/Primedia Productions/Primetime Television Co-Production

8.30 A Week in Politics
PETER JAY
Every Friday night, Channel Four's own political magazine takes a fresh look at the ideas, issues and personalities of British politics with presenter Peter Jay and reporters Emily McFarquhar and Vivian White.
STUDIO DIRECTOR MIKE LLOYD
PRODUCTION
DAVID ASH, LEA SELLERS
PRODUCER ANNE LAPPING
EXECUTIVE PRODUCER
DAVID ELSTEIN
Brook Productions

9.15 Ladybirds — Elaine Page
Elaine Page decided at an early age to make acting her career and set out to make her wish come true. Her bonus was the truly beautiful singing voice which soared out of this diminutive girl to lead her through a series of West End shows culminating in her triumphant *Evita* and *Cats*. Tonight Elaine tells her story and reminds us in song of some of her favourite moments.
See page 4
CAMERA ANDREW PARKINSON
DIRECTOR MIKE MANSFIELD
ASSOCIATE PRODUCER
HILARY STEWART
PRODUCER MURIEL YOUNG
EXECUTIVE PRODUCER
MIKE MANSFIELD
Mike Mansfield Enterprises Production

BBC1   BBC2

5.40 pm
Evening News
with **Moira Stuart**
including a report on the
Liberal Party Assembly
Weatherman

6.5 Regional
news magazines
Look East, Look North
Look North West, Midlands Today
South East at Six
Points West, South Today
Spotlight South West

(Regional details as Monday)

6.30 *New series*
Friday Sportstime
A new programme in which the
BBC's sports commentators and
reporters bring you action, the
news, the stories behind the news,
expert comment and informed
opinion.
Introduced by **Desmond Lynam**

Producer JIM RESIDE
Editor BOB ABRAHAMS

6.50 Banjo
The Woodpile Cat
An animated film
When Banjo's mischief at home
earns him a spanking from his Pa,
he stows away in a truck to the
big city. But a homesick Banjo
finds even more trouble there than
back on the farm!

A DON BLUTH production

7.15-8.45
The Brides of Fu Manchu
continues a short season of films
starring **Christopher Lee** as the
master criminal Fu Manchu with
Douglas Wilmer as Nayland Smith.
At his secret headquarters in
North Africa, Dr Fu Manchu
holds captive 12 beautiful girls.
Each of them is related to an in-
fluential figure whose collaboration
he hopes to obtain to further his
plan to dominate the world . . .

8.45 pm
Points of View
Barry Took with your comments
in the programme you help to
write.

Please send letters to Barry Took, BBC
Television Centre, London W12 8QT.
Producer CAROL WHITE

9.0 pm
Nine O'Clock News
with
Sue Lawley
and the BBC's reporters and
correspondents around the world
Weekend Weather
MICHAEL FISH

5.10
Mass Communication
James Bond: 8
This programme observes the ad-
vertising and publicity campaign
for the James Bond film *The Spy
Who Loved Me*. It contains parts
of the marketing meetings at
United Artists' London office.

Producer VICTOR LOCKWOOD
A BBC/Open University production
(Repeat)

5.35 Weekend-Outlook
helps you plan your weekend by
previewing daytime programmes
of special interest from the Open
University. This week's selection
includes: *Three Families: Jeru-
salem, New Tyres from Old?* and
Montgeoffroy: Life in a Château.

Producer KEVIN NEWPORT
A BBC/Open University production

5.40-7.0
The Friday Western:
The Raid
starring **Van Heflin**
with **Anne Bancroft**
Richard Boone, Lee Marvin
Van Heflin leads a group of es-
caped Confederate soldiers who
systematically plan the sacking
of a small Vermont town to avenge
the burning of Atlanta. Based
upon an actual incident of the
Civil War, this tense and exciting
Western drama is given superb
support by Anne Bancroft, Richard Boone and Lee Marvin.

Major Neal Benton.....VAN HEFLIN
Katy Bishop.........ANNE BANCROFT
Captain Foster......RICHARD BOONE
Lieut Keating............LEE MARVIN
Larry Bishop..........TOMMY RETTIG
Captain Dwyer.........PETER GRAVES
The Rev Lucas...DOUGLAS SPENCER
Col Tucker............PAUL CAVANAGH
Banker Anderson......WILL WRIGHT
Corporal Dean.........JOHN DIERKES
Delphine Coates.........HELEN FORD
Mr Danzig................HARRY HINES
Capt Henderson.........SIMON SCOTT
Lieut Ramsey..........CLAUDE AKINS

Screenplay by SIDNEY BOEHM
Produced by ROBERT L. JACKS
Directed by HUGO FREGONESE
Films: page 22

7.0 pm
Cartoon Two
The Three Knights
Three knights set out to fulfil their
individual dreams with the best
intentions, and desire to right all
wrongs, but instead they leave
behind them a trail of havoc and
destruction.

Written and directed by MARK BAKER of
West Surrey College of Art and Design.

7.10 Jack High
*The Kodak Masters Bowls
Tournament*
from Beach House Park, Worthing
The original eight world-class flat
green bowlers are now down to
the four semi-finalists. With the
stands packed at Worthing from
the early morning, nobody was
disappointed by the standard of
bowls in this first semi-final.
Commentators
DAVID VINE, DAVID RHYS JONES

Producer JOHNNIE WATHERSTON

7.40 Civilisation
A personal view by **Kenneth Clark**
13: *Heroic Materialism*
In this, the final programme,
Kenneth Clark shows how the
heroic materialism of the past
hundred years has been linked
with an equally remarkable
increase in humanitarianism. The
achievement of engineers and
scientists – Brunel and Rutherford,
for example – has been matched
by that of the great reformers like
Wilberforce and Shaftesbury.
KENNETH CLARK's thoughts on the
period in which we are now living
took him from the English indus-
trial landscapers of the contem-
porary New York, the world of the
radio telescope and the exploration of space.

Produced by MICHAEL GILL
and PETER MONTAGNON (Repeat)
★ Subtitles on Ceefax page 270

8.35-9.0
Gardeners' World
from
Swansea Botanic Gardens
Which are the best trees and
shrubs to use as hedging?
What herbaceous plants can we
use for autumn flowering, and how
can we build a rock garden for
acidic and calcareous plants? Just
some of the topical ideas which
Geoff Hamilton discusses with
Harry Parker.

Executive producer JOHN KENYON
Production assistant JEAN LAUGHTON
Producer DENIS W. GARTSIDE
BBC Pebble Mill
*Summary of gardening tips on
Ceefax page 268*

The Three Knights 7.0 pm BBC2

33 Maps: regions

When you are looking for a place on a map you need to know about REGIONS. Look at this map of an island:

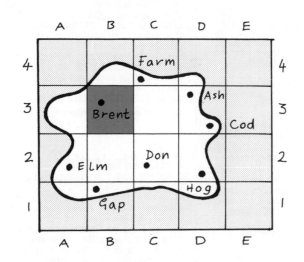

You can find out where a place is by reading its ADDRESS. Brent's address is B3 – this means it is in the REGION where column B and row 3 meet. Region B3 is coloured in blue on the map.

1. Write down the addresses of the other places shown on the map. Remember – the **letter** goes first in the address!
2. List the towns in alphabetical order.
3. What do you notice?

34

Look at this map:

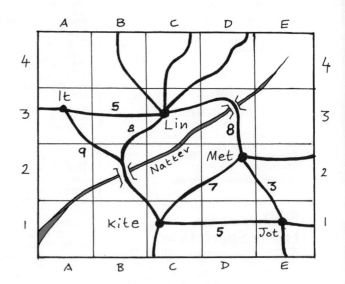

Distances between towns are marked in kilometres.

Look at the information on the map and answer these questions:

1. Give the addresses of the two bridges][.
2. Starting at Kite, work out the total distance in kilometres of a 'round trip' to all the towns, travelling anti-clockwise.
3. Write down all the towns' addresses in the order you would go through them:

   Kite (C1), Jot ____

4. You want to go from Jot to Lin. Is it quicker to go through Kite or Met? How do you know?
5. In which region does the River Natter begin? What does this tell you about the height of the land in that region?
6. Where on the map can you see a likely place for a traffic jam? What makes you think so?
7. Which is the most important town? What clues on the map tell you this?
8. If the bus travels at 20 km/hour, how long will it take to get from Kite to Jot?

35 Maps: directions

Look at this map:

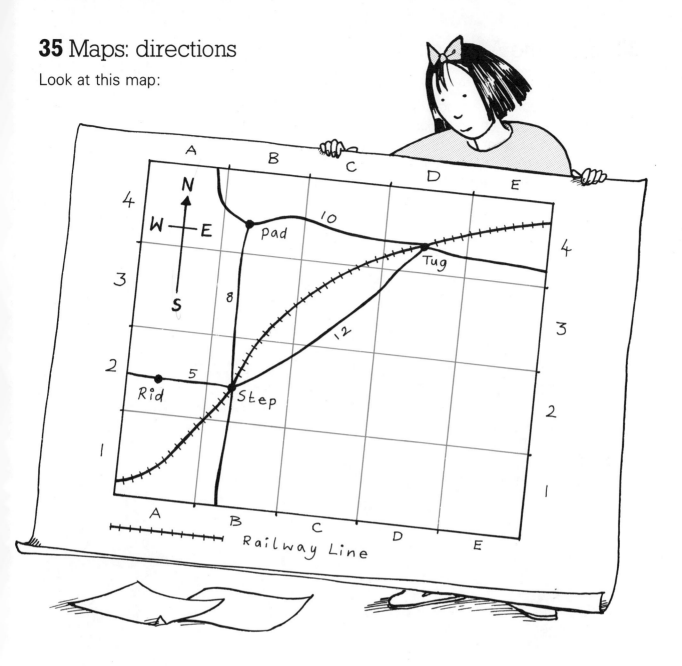

Distances in miles between towns are marked.

The N arrow tells you that if you are going in the same direction as the arrow, you are travelling **North**.

1. What do the other three direction letters stand for?
2. If you travel from Step to Rid, in which **direction** are you going?
3. If you travel South from Pad, which town will you come to?
4. If you travel West for 10 miles from Tug, then turn South and travel 8 miles, which town will you reach?
5. If you wanted to get from Step to Tug, which way is the quickest – road or rail? What makes you think so?
6. If you arrive in Step from the South, do you turn left or right along the road to Rid?
7. How far is it from Rid to Tug?
8. Give the names of the two railway stations and their map addresses.
9. You start out from Rid and head East. At the next town you meet a large roundabout with three exits. You take the second exit and travel to the next town. When you arrive there you turn West and travel for ten miles. Where are you now? How far have you travelled?
10. If you are facing a road sign showing Step to the left and Pad to the right, where are you?

36 Maps: the AA Service atlas

The *AA Handbook* has a road atlas section at the back. Like other road atlases, you find the map you want by looking at the 'key', which is a map of the whole of Britain, divided into rectangular sections. The numbers inside each rectangle tell you the page on which you will find a detailed map of that area. Some much smaller areas, like large cities, have a whole page to themselves in the map section.

Here is the atlas key from one edition of the *AA Handbook*:

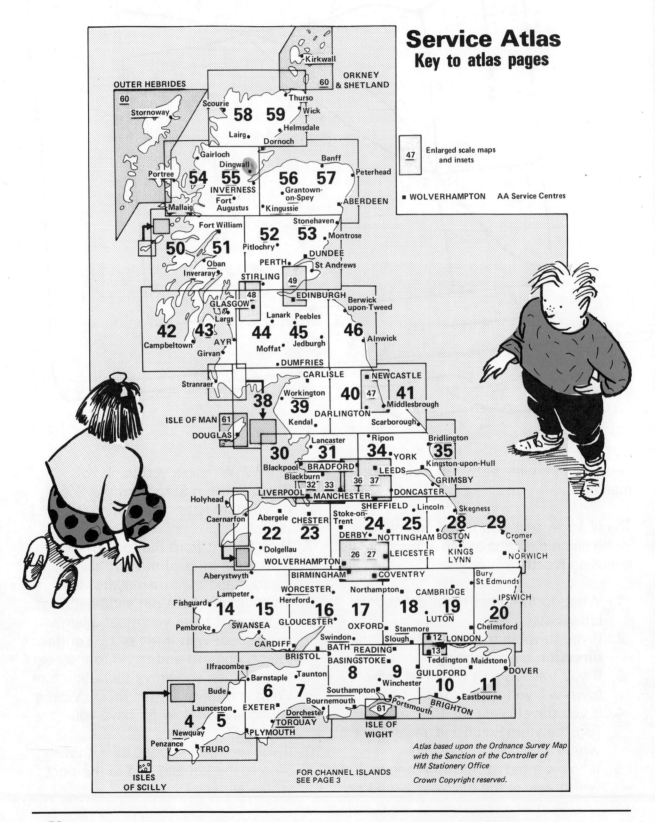

Service Atlas
Key to atlas pages

| 47 | Enlarged scale maps and insets |

■ WOLVERHAMPTON   AA Service Centres

Atlas based upon the Ordnance Survey Map with the Sanction of the Controller of HM Stationery Office

Crown Copyright reserved.

FOR CHANNEL ISLANDS
SEE PAGE 3

Answer these questions:

1. How many map pages are shown on this atlas key?
2. On which pages will you find maps of:
   a) Glasgow?
   b) London?
   c) Newcastle?
   d) Edinburgh?
   e) Birmingham?
3. Which other area of Britain shares a page with the Isle of Wight?
4. Is the Isle of Wight in the north or south of this map?
5. On which page will you find the Channel Islands?
6. On which page will you find the Isles of Scilly?

7. Which town on this map is furthest north?
8. Which large town will you find on page 32?
9. Why are some towns written in block capitals?
10. Write down the numbers of the pages on which you will find maps showing these towns:
    a) Dover
    b) Truro
    c) Swansea
    d) Norwich
    e) York
    f) Southampton
    g) Aberdeen
    h) Chester
    i) Inverness
    j) Oxford

37 Using a road map

Here is a section from the map pages in the *AA Handbook*, showing the area around Norwich:

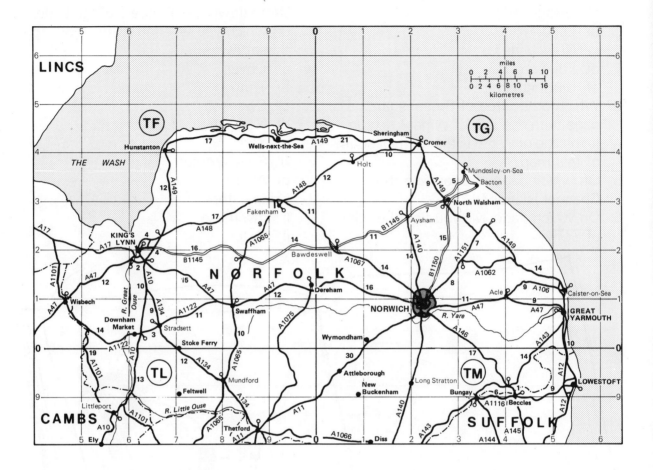

County names are in large block capitals.
Important towns are in block capitals.
Other towns are written in ordinary type.
Road numbers (such as A47) are shown beside the roads.
Distances in miles are given between places marked with a 'pin' ⚲

Use the information on the map to answer these questions:

1. What is the largest town shown on the map?
2. Which county occupies most of the map?
3. What is the stretch of water north of King's Lynn called?
4. If you travel from Norwich to Great Yarmouth, in which direction are you going?

5. If you want to go from Great Yarmouth to Lowestoft,
   a) which road will you use?
   b) how far is it?
   c) in which direction will you be travelling?
6. How far is it from:
   a) Norwich to Dereham?
   b) Lowestoft to Beccles?
   c) Norwich to North Walsham?
   d) Dereham to Swaffham?
   e) North Walsham to Cromer?
   f) Fakenham to Holt?
   g) Wisbech to Downham Market?
   h) Great Yarmouth to Norwich?
7. To work out your last answer what did you have to do?
8. Which road would you travel on from:
   a) Norwich to Wymondham?

b) Beccles to Bungay?
c) Swaffham to Dereham?
d) Cromer to Sheringham?
e) Downham Market to Ely?
f) North Walsham to Mundesley-on-Sea?
g) Fakenham to King's Lynn?

9. Which river reaches the sea at King's Lynn?

10. Make a list of the roads you would use and the total distance you would travel if you went from:

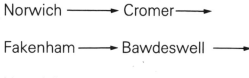

Norwich ⟶ Cromer ⟶

Fakenham ⟶ Bawdeswell ⟶

Norwich.

38 Map references

To give someone the exact 'address' of a town, you need to look at the **grid lines** (squares) which cover the map.

This is the 'address' or **map reference** for Norwich:

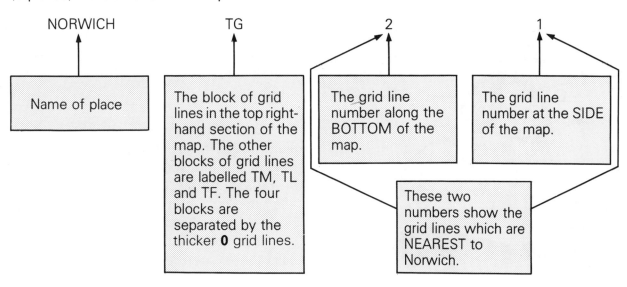

NORWICH	TG	2	1
Name of place	The block of grid lines in the top right-hand section of the map. The other blocks of grid lines are labelled TM, TL and TF. The four blocks are separated by the thicker **0** grid lines.	The grid line number along the BOTTOM of the map.	The grid line number at the SIDE of the map.

These two numbers show the grid lines which are NEAREST to Norwich.

So Norwich's map reference is **TG 21**.

When you write the last two digits (the nearest grid lines), the grid line on the BOTTOM of the map is always written first!

BRAIN BOX

1. Use the information on the map in exercise 38 to write down the map references of these towns:
   a) North Walsham
   b) Cromer
   c) King's Lynn
   d) Downham Market
   e) Beccles

2. Which towns will you find near these map references?
   a) TG 10   f) TF 81
   b) TG 41   g) TF 70
   c) TL 79   h) TF 74
   d) TG 01   i) TM 29
   e) TM 19   j) TF 93

39 Planning a road journey

You will need your own copy of the *AA Handbook* and you will need to use the road maps, the breakdown service information and the gazetteer section.

First of all, find the map showing the area around Gloucester.

Using the information on the map and in the other sections of the handbook, make a diary and route plan to show this weekend excursion to the Cotswolds. Include **every detail** – road numbers, place names, telephone numbers, hotel names, garages etc.

Look in the Contents page to find all these.

AA Handbook

Your family live in Oxford and you all decide to spend the weekend in Gloucestershire. You leave Oxford on Friday evening at 1830, taking the A40 westward. After travelling for half an hour at an average speed of 44 mph, you turn south on the next 'A' road and drive for a further nine miles before stopping to have some crisps at the local pub in the town.

You then turn west on to the A417 and travel for thirteen miles. You stop there for the night, staying in the 3-star hotel.

On Saturday morning you set off on the A429, travelling north. After ten miles you stop off to look around the village.

You continue along the A429 and stop at the next village for lunch, which you eat at the two-star pub and hotel.

Your journey continues along the A429 until you reach the next town, where you turn on to the A424, heading north. After travelling for 15 minutes at 40 mph you stop for a look around the village. You spend the rest of the afternoon there, and have tea at the hotel on The Green. You decide to book in there for Saturday night.

On Sunday morning you set off south along the A46, turning left along the 'B' road at the first road junction. You stop at the second place marked on the map and have coffee at the hotel in The Square. When Mum tries to start the car, she finds the electrics have failed, so she calls the AA centre in Gloucester. They can't fix the car on the spot, so they call the garage in Chipping Norton. The car is towed there and it takes until 3 o'clock to repair it.

From there you travel back to Oxford along the shortest route.

Present your diary and route plan in an interesting way. Here is one idea for the basic route plan:

From	Road used	To	Distance (miles)	Hotel names	Garages/ Service centres
1. Oxford	A40				
2.					
3.					

40 Map references: world atlas

To find a place in an atlas, you must first look it up in the **index** at the back. If you were looking for Tel Aviv you might find it listed like this:

The **map reference** for Tel Aviv is:

22

The page in the atlas on which you will find the map.

B   3

The letter and number show the REGION on the map where you will find Tel Aviv.

On atlas page 22 you will see that the map has a row of letters at the top and bottom, and a series of numbers at the sides:

	A	B	C	D	E	
5						5
4						4
3		▨				3
2						2
1						1
	A	B	C	D	E	

Tel Aviv will be found in map region B3 (the region has been shaded in to show you).

Use the index of your classroom atlas to write down the map references of these places:

1. Amsterdam
2. Cape Canaveral
3. Delhi
4. Florence
5. Hamburg
6. San Marino
7. Trafalgar
8. Zambezi River
9. Yangtze-Kiang
10. Montevideo

41

Look at this outline map of the Middle East:

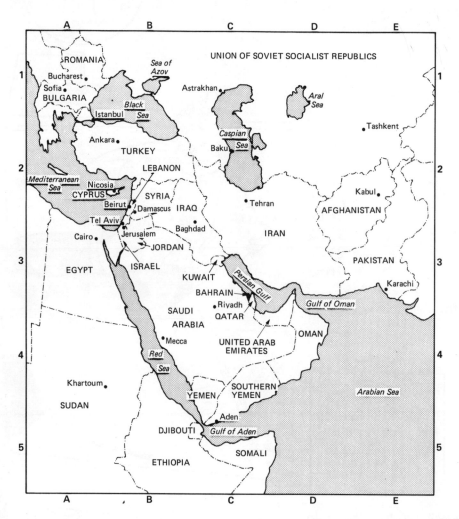

Look at the grid letters and numbers, then give the map references for these places:

1. Cyprus
2. Istanbul
3. Baku
4. Karachi
5. Tashkent
6. Tehran
7. Cairo
8. Mecca
9. Kabul
10. Astrakhan
11. Sea of Azov
12. Aden
13. Bahrain
14. Beirut
15. Baghdad

42

Use the index of your classroom atlas to find the map references for these places. Find each place in the atlas and write down the name of the country you found it in:

1. Sakhalin
2. Lhasa
3. Zagreb
4. Monterey
5. São Paulo
6. Harare
7. Cork
8. Kinshasa
9. Riga
10. Göteborg
11. Beira
12. Hobart
13. Georgetown
14. Houston
15. Guantánamo

43 Contour shading

Some maps show how high the land is by using different colours for different heights – these are called **relief** maps. The **contours** are the lines between different heights. Look at this map:

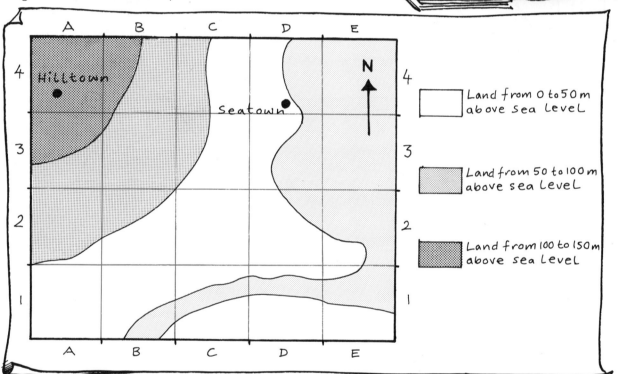

1. How high is the land near the sea?
2. If there are cliffs near the sea, what is the highest they could be?
3. If you go from Seatown to Hilltown are you travelling downhill or uphill?
4. About how much higher is Hilltown than Seatown?
5. If the scale of the map is 1 cm to 1 kilometre, how far is it from Seatown to Hilltown?
6. Estimate how long a bus would take to go from Seatown to Hilltown if it travelled at 30 km per hour.
7. Why might the bus be quicker coming back to Seatown?
8. In which direction is the river flowing?
9. How many **contour lines** are there on the map?
10. Give the map references for:
    a) Seatown
    b) Hilltown
    c) the mouth of the river

44

Look at this map:

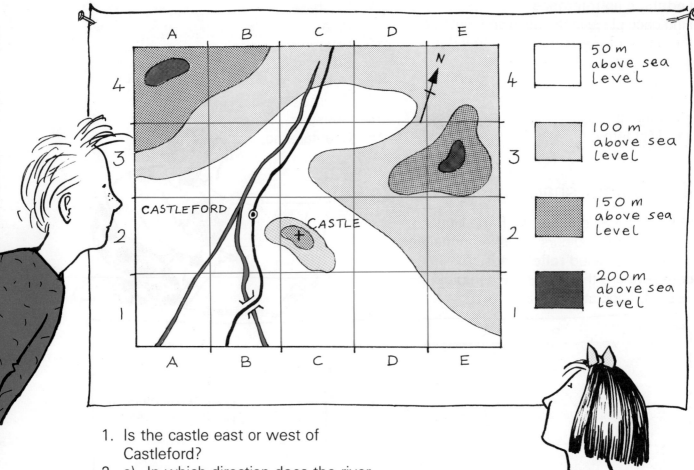

1. Is the castle east or west of Castleford?
2. a) In which direction does the river flow?
   b) What information on the map tells you this?
3. In which region does the river divide into two?
4. In which regions is the highest land?
5. If you travel from Castleford towards the nearest high ground, in which direction are you going?
6. Why do you think the castle was built where it is? (Two reasons.)
7. a) How high is the hill on which the castle stands?
   b) How much higher is it than the town?
8. What do you think the name 'Castleford' means? (Clue – look up 'ford' in the dictionary.)
9. Why do you think the town was not built on the other side of the river?
10. Why does the road which goes north from Castleford follow the line of the river? (Clue – look at the contours.)

45 Using relief maps

Use the index of your classroom atlas to find these regions. Look at the contour shading and give their approximate height:

1. Scandinavian Highland – over 1000 metres.
2. Gran Chaco
3. Sierra Nevada
4. Siberian Plateau
5. Pyrenees
6. Gibson Desert
7. Kalahari Desert
8. Patagonia
9. Central Russian Uplands
10. Nullarbor Plain
11. Zaïre Basin
12. Great Plains
13. Ural Mountains
14. Anatolian Plateau
15. North China Plain

Find these mountains in your atlas and give their exact height in metres:

16. Mont Blanc
17. Mount Bruce
18. Mount Chimborazo
19. Mount Olympus
20. Mount Cook
21. Mount McKinley
22. Ben Nevis
23. Mount Fujiyama
24. Jebel Toubkal
25. Mount Roraima

Use a map of Great Britain to answer these questions:

1. Look at the scale of the map. How many kilometres does 1 cm stand for?
2. Use the scale and a ruler to work out the distance in km from:
   a) London to Dublin
   b) London to Glasgow
   c) Belfast to London
   d) Birmingham to Southampton

46

Use your classroom atlas to answer these questions:

1. In which country in Africa are the Tibesti Mountains?
2. Jakarta is the capital of _____.
3. Mount Aconcagua is _____ metres high and is on the border between _____ and _____.
4. _____ is the capital of Chile.
5. The West Indies are islands in the _____ Sea.
6. Blue Mountain Peak is the highest mountain in _____.
7. The country next to Haiti is _____.
8. Name the six countries which border the USSR in Europe.
9. Which country owns the Faeroe Islands?
10. Sri Lanka is a large island south of _____.
11. Laos is between _____ and _____.
12. Afghanistan is south of _____.
13. The USA and USSR are separated by a stretch of water called the _____ _____.
14. The capital of the USA is _____. It is on the _____ coast of America.
15. The railway from Londonderry to Ballymena goes via _____.

3. The Isle of Man lies between _____ and _____.
4. The islands furthest north are the _____.
5. Cardigan Bay is part of _____.
6. The Wicklow Mountains are in _____.
7. Berwick-upon-Tweed is on the border between _____ and _____.
8. What do you notice about the roads and railways around London?
9. What is the name of the most southerly part of Dorset?
10. In which counties will you find these towns? (Look up their map references in the index to help you find them.)
    a) Middlesbrough
    b) Barnstaple
    c) Skegness
    d) Prestatyn
    e) Kenilworth
    f) Omagh
    g) Peterhead
    h) Livingston

48 Gathering geographical and historical information

You will need to use an atlas, an encyclopedia and non-fiction books to answer these questions:

1. a) What is the population of the United States?
   b) When did it become an independent country?
   c) When did the American Civil War begin?
   d) Who burnt Atlanta during this war?
   e) In which state of the USA is Atlanta?
   f) Which mountain range reaches south to Atlanta?
   g) Which river reaches the sea at New Orleans?
   h) How long is it?
   i) Near which of the Great Lakes is Detroit?
   j) Which industry is concentrated there?
   k) In which state is Salt Lake City?
   l) Which religious organisation has its headquarters there?
   m) Which industry is sited in Galveston?
   n) In which state is it?
   o) In which country is the Gulf of California?

2. a) What is the capital of Finland?
   b) Which three countries does it share borders with?
   c) Ships travelling from the North Sea to Finland pass through a narrow strait between _____ and _____.
   d) Why is sea travel difficult from Helsinki in January?
   e) Who is the president of Finland?
   f) Who did the Finns fight against from 1939 to 1940?
   g) Who was their leader at that time?
   h) What is the region in the north of Finland called?
   i) Which animal do the people of that region depend on?

j) Which Soviet town lies directly opposite Helsinki?
k) Which town does the road which runs east from Helsinki reach?
l) When did the natural gas pipeline from the USSR begin operations?
m) What is another main source of power used in Finland?
n) How much of Finland is used for farming?
o) Which famous composer was a Finn?

49 Grid references

This is to remind you how to write down the **address** or **map reference** of a place. Look at this map:

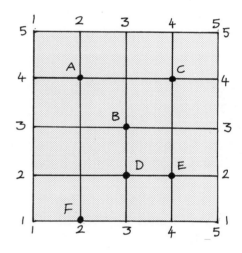

To write A's address (map reference) you look first at the TOP or BOTTOM numbers. A is on vertical grid line number 2. Then look at the SIDE numbers. A is on horizontal grid line number 4.

So A's address (**grid reference**) is: 24

Write down the grid references for:

1. B
2. C
3. D
4. E
5. F

50 The National Grid

Look at this map:

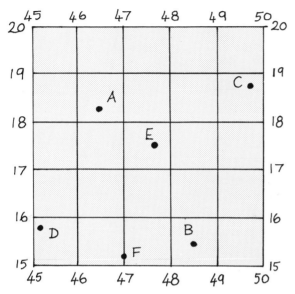

To give the grid reference for the places marked, you first need to look at the grid line numbers on the TOP or BOTTOM. (They are called 'eastings' because you count across from west to east.)

One problem – place A is **between** eastings (grid lines) 46 and 47! So you have to estimate how many **tenths** A is between 46 and 47.

It looks about 5 tenths (5/10) further on from easting 46. So the first part of its grid reference is:

> 465 (which means easting 46 and
> 5 more tenths)

Now you look at the SIDE numbers. (They are called 'northings' because you count upwards from south to north.)

Another problem – A is **between** northings 18 and 19! So you have to estimate how many **tenths** A is between 18 and 19.

It looks about 3 tenths (3/10) further on from northing 18. So the second part of its grid reference is:

> 183 (which means northing 18 and
> 3 more tenths)

> So A's **full** six-number reference is
> **4 6 5 1 8 3**

1. Write down the grid references for: B, C, D, E and F.
2. Were there any tenths after easting 47 for F? (If the place is right on a grid line you have to write **0** in the tenths space, so that the reference has still got six numbers.)

51 Using grid references

Look at this section from an Ordnance
Survey map:

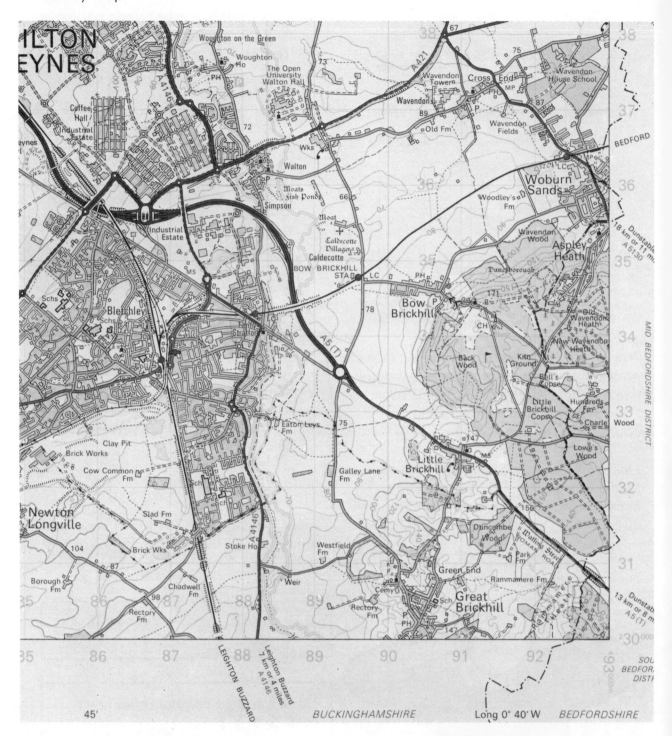

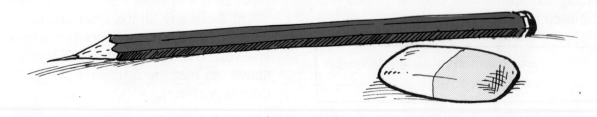

Give the grid references for these places:

1. Bow Brickhill Station
2. Woodley's Farm
3. Galley Lane Farm
4. The weir on the Grand Union Canal
5. Woburn Sands Station

What will you find at these grid references?

6. 909373
7. 912344
8. 891311
9. 886371
10. 906305
11. 865322
12. 893335
13. 924334
14. 884329
15. 905368

The scale of this map is 1:50,000. This means that one centimetre on the map stands for 50,000 cm on the ground.

16. How much is that in:
   a) metres?
   b) kilometres?

17. Use your ruler to work out the real 'direct' distances between these places on the map. Give your answers in kilometres.
   a) Bow Brickhill Station and Woburn Sands Station
   b) Westfield Farm and Little Brickhill church
   c) 856307 and 865322
   d) 906305 and 893336
   e) 911325 and 916369
18. If you travel from 893335 to 893322, in which direction are you travelling?
19. Use an Ordnance Survey map to find out what the symbols at these grid references mean:
   a) 908371
   b) 908323
   c) 928354
   d) 901308
   e) 913337
   f) 893354
   g) 913342
   h) 915343
   i) 927337
   j) 904348
20. The contour lines on the map give the height in metres above sea level. How high are these points?
   a) 893335
   b) 924334
   c) 856308

Index

The numbers refer to the exercise, not the page.